STRUCK

STRUCK

GEOFFREY W. BROMHEAD

Anvil Press | Vancouver | 2003

Anvil Press
6 West 17th Avenue
Vancouver, B.C.
V5Y 1Z4

NATIONAL LIBRARY OF CANADA CATALOGUING IN PUBLICATION DATA

Bromhead, Geoffrey, 1979-
Struck / Geoffrey Bromhead.

Winner of the 25th Annual 3-Day Novel-Writing Contest"—t.p.
ISBN: 1-895636-53-1

I. Title
PS8553.R6345S77 2003   C813'.6   C2003-911019-2

Printed and bound in Canada
Book and cover design: HeimatHouse

Represented in Canada by the Literary Press Group
Distributed by The University of Toronto Press

Anvil Press gratefully acknowledges the support of The Canada
Council for the Arts, The B.C. Arts Council, and the Book
Publishing Industry Development Program of the
Department of Canadian Heritage.

I saw a man pursuing the horizon;
Round and round they sped.
I was disturbed at this;
I accosted the man.
"It is futile," I said,
"You can never—"

"You lie," he cried,
And ran on.

— Stephen Crane, 1895

I

LIGHTNING FRACTURES THE SKY. A blue luminescence traces the edges of clouds, then flickers away, followed by a low rumbling and a sharp crack. Rain courses down pine trees, releasing the smell of fresh sap into the charged air. Finnigan Heller puts his sunglasses on as he waits to be struck by lightning for the sixteenth time.

Finnigan stands twelve-and-a-half metres from an eight-metre-high pine tree, the highest object in the area. He spreads his hands out and turns his head to the sky, watching. A tingling at the bottom of his spine marks the instant before contact. It moves like a serpent up his body, reaching his neck, then splitting to each shoulder, down each arm, settling in the palms of his hands. The charge moves through his pelvis, down his legs, swirls about his ankles, and builds in his arches. His jaw begins to quiver, and Finnigan can feel the electricity in his sinuses making his eyes water.

The bolt hits just under his left shoulderblade, searing through his body to the ground, heaving him nine metres across the field. He slides along several more metres of wet grass before he comes to rest. Finnigan is spread-eagled on the ground, and before he loses consciousness, he smiles.

Eric Able arrives at the Toronto International Airport at 2:36 a.m. After telling the plump flight attendant that he would rather eat her for dinner than the poor excuse for barbecued chicken, he found himself rather hungry. The drink she "accidentally" spilled on him stained his light grey suit a peculiar shade of blue around the collar.

Pastel colours bathe the food court, making it look more like a stage set than a place to eat. The fast-food establishments are built into a miniature simulacrum of an urban neighbourhood, complete with iron fire escapes and red brick walls. The heavy, greasy smell of french fries and pizza tie Eric Able's stomach into fierce knots. After some searching, he finds a steak restaurant far from the food court. He orders shrimp and lobster and a vodka on ice.

The vodka is cheap, but agreeable. He places his brief-case on the chair next to him, and his mouth waters as he thumbs the combination for each latch. As the latches snap open, he breathes in sharply through his mouth, a wave of excitement rippling through his chest and stom-ach. Inside the briefcase is a thick yellow folder, the edges worn with age. Eric Able's fingers run across the surface of the folder before he lifts it out and sets it on the table. The tab on the upper-right corner of the folder is labelled Subject: Finnigan Heller. Eric Able licks his lips as he reads the name.

The waiter sets the plate on the table. "Shrimp and lobster. Can I get you anything else?"

Eric Able ignores the food and the waiter, and opens the folder. He has memorized every word on every page, every photograph, every statistic, every coffee stain and every crease. The folder is in his memory, yet he is stimulated whenever he is in its physical presence, when he can smell it, touch it. Only in these times can he *know* it.

He touches behind his lower lip with his middle finger and feels the moisture there. A small bead of saliva forms at his fingertip and begins to slide down his lip. His eyes move over the words, cementing them in his mind as if for the first time. The shrimp and lobster go cold and uneaten.

A blunt, two-storey building hunkers in the morning rain, windows shuddering beneath the intermittent thunder-claps. The heavy raindrops stain the pale sandstone walls the colour of charcoal, and as Penelope Mason struggles through the parking lot, she thinks the building looks like a lump of coal submerged in a puddle. She passes into the building with a sigh and folds her umbrella as she walks down a long hallway to the back stairs. Ever since her office was transferred to this building two months ago, Mason has gone out of her way to avoid the main elevators and staircase, for those are the prime stalking grounds of one Clyde Willem, field agent.

Willem, a tree trunk of a man, smelled Mason walk through the front door on her first day in the building. Not knowing any better, Mason was polite to the lumbering former cop. Willem, taking Mason's politeness as an invitation, asked her to dinner after knowing her for twenty minutes. Mason declined, and since then, plans her day around avoiding Willem and all of his known hunting grounds: the main elevator, the decaying cafeteria, and the first-floor water fountain. On an unlucky day, which happens at least once a week, Willem finds himself in the basement offices, by accident, and pokes his head into Mason's research area "just to say hi."

"He's like, 6'4", Mom," Mason says into the phone on her desk. "He's a concrete pillar, and about as smart as one, too."

"Hmmm. I guess the smart ones don't work for the government, do they?"

"Certainly not," replies Mason, aware of the implication on her own intelligence. Mason half listens to her mother, and skims the morning newspaper while steam rises from a mug of coffee on the edge of her desk. Mason's mother sits at home most mornings and smokes cigarettes and talks to her daughter on the phone. Her asthmatic voice crackles and strains on the other end of the line.

"Well, you can just have dinner with me then," her mother says.

"I'm busy all this week, Mom. I'm still moving things into my new office."

"Still? You've been there for two months already."

"There's a lot going on here, Mom," Mason lies. On page two of the paper, right next to the week's weather forecast, Mason's eyes focus on a headline, and her mother's voice joins the rest of the ambient noise in the room. The headline reads, *Windsor Man Survives Lightning Strike*. Mason scans the rest of the article until she finds what she's looking for.

"Penelope? Are you there?" asks her mother.

"Mom, I have to go." Mason sets the receiver down and folds the newspaper around so she can focus on the article. She reads it again, then opens a metal drawer in her desk. The large drawer, a cornucopia of old folders and reports, half-completed studies and forgotten proposals for new ones, fills Mason with disorganized despair. After working for seven years as a research scientist for Canadian Intelligence, her grant funding was not renewed, and budget cuts forced her into the forsaken office building she now occupies. Mason is now one of six scientists working in the building, none of them on a coordinated project, each of them awaiting word on who loses his or her job next.

Before she lost her grant, Mason studied the psychological effects of severe weather patterns in Canada, specifically areas that experience drastic weather changes over a short period of time. During those seven years, Mason came across an unusual weather phenomenon in the form of a man named Finnigan Heller. His is the name she sees in the newspaper article now, and the name she searches for in the depths of the metal desk drawer. She knocks her mug over as she clears a space on her desk for the folder. The coffee fans out as the mug tumbles through the air, reaching as far as the desk next to hers. The heavy ceramic mug survives the fall except for a large, half-moon shaped chip along the rim. "Fuck," she mutters. She picks up the mug and the curved fragment from the polished ceramic tile floor. The pool of coffee collects in the cracks between the tiles. The coffee that made it to the desk next to hers drips to the floor, joining the rest of the puddle.

Mason turns back to her desk and the thin folder marked only with the name Finnigan Heller. The folder is just a collection of newspaper articles, only half of which mention Heller by name. A picture, photocopied from a high school yearbook, is interlaced with grey and white lines obscuring the face and rendering the likeness nearly useless. Also on a well-used sheet of paper are Mason's notes on Heller: how often he's been struck that she knows about, his birthplace, his homes since child-hood, and the known locations of his lightning strikes. Mason tried once to calculate the odds of one man being hit that many times, and the calculator couldn't handle the number. For one man to have so much energy con-centrated around him that the laws of nature are strained to the fullest compels her. No, seven years ago it was compelling, now her life centres on these first minutes of her day, looking in the newspaper for the time when he is close enough to her that she is caught in his gravity. Mason lost track of Heller more than a year ago after a hit in Winnipeg, and now he's as close as Windsor.

"Dr. Mason? We're sending Jack out for some dough-nuts. You want anything?" Dr. Alison leans in the doorway of the shared office space. Mason just sits and stares at the file, fingering the photo of Heller. Dr. Alison pushes her black-rimmed glasses up her nose and clears her throat. "Dr. Mason?"

Mason looks up and says, "I spilled some coffee on the side of your desk." Dr. Alison furrows her brow and looks across the top of her desk to make sure that no coffee has stained any of her papers. She bites back a frustrated sigh; every day of the last two months working with Dr. Mason has been an extreme exercise in patience. The other researchers in the building dismissed Mason as odd and kept out of her way, but Dr. Alison has tried to be friendly, despite her new co-worker's reclusive behavior. Mason grabs a newspaper and a folder from her desk and hurries out of the room while Dr. Alison searches for something to clean up the mess.

A rogue sunbeam struggles through the thick clouds into Clyde Willem's office. Tiny particles, seemingly trapped within the sunbeam, swirl from the window to his desk. The rain still falls, and Willem watches by the window with his arms crossed over his thick chest. He squints against the sunbeam, and feels dirty as the dust collects on his shoulders. The dust disturbs the order of the room, an order that requires constant dusting and polishing to maintain. He sighs in frustration, since he cleaned and polished the entire office only the day before.

He crouches to the black nylon duffel bag beside the desk, and hoists the strap over his shoulder. Lunch is still a while away, but he can't stand the disorder of the dust in his office. The building's only redeeming feature is the full gym on the first floor. Much of the budget must have been spent in that room alone; clearly Canadian Intelligence agents are meant to look good, even if there aren't very many of them. In the weight room is where Clyde Willem is confident; it is the one place where he is respected, even admired. His musculature is a work of art: strong and formidable, yet lean and agile. In the gym, Clyde Willem is in control. In his office, he has no control, especially whenever he sees Penelope Mason walk in the door.

The snobby scientist who was shoehorned into the basement offices two months ago started off agreeable, even pleasant, but became the office hermit after a family crisis forced her to excuse herself from a dinner invitation.

Willem stands with his back to the window, looking at Mason standing in the doorway with a newspaper and manila folder. One hand rests on her hip. Her plain black hair is drawn up in a tight bun, pulling the skin around her eyes into thin slits. At almost six feet, Mason is the only woman in the building that Willem finds tall enough to suit him, but otherwise her physical attributes fail to impress him, except for her stunning nose. He looks at it now, straight on, and admires its perfect proportion, its elegant symmetry, and regrets that an equally beautiful face does not accompany it.

She steps over the threshold, straightens her navy blue suit jacket with her free hand and attempts a friendly, but not-too-friendly, smile. It fails when she tries showing her teeth, looking more like a cornered dog than a cordial co-worker. "Willem, I need something from you."

"Of course you do."

Mason puts the folder and the newspaper down on the desk. She turns her head slightly to the left, allowing Willem to admire her nose in profile. The bridge appears to be straight, but after examining it many times, Willem has found that it is actually a very gentle parabola, curving from brow to the tip almost imperceptibly.

"I need to do some field work."

Willem pulls back the black upholstered chair from his desk and eases his large frame into the squeaking seat, dropping his gym bag on the floor beside him. He returns Mason's attempted smile with one of his own. "Too bad you're not a field agent. You know that needs papers, and signatures, and all kinds of authorizations."

"Not if you come with me."

Willem leans back in his chair and drums his finger-tips against each other. "Look, Mason, I don't have time to waste on your silly weather projects. I have a number of important cases I'm working on right now..."

"Don't embarrass yourself, Willem. There are no important cases. If there were, the intelligence budget would include more than your salary and the birdseed that feeds the hamster spinning the wheel inside your head. This is important."

"It must be, since you're being so nice about it. But I'll bite. What little science fair project have you got that requires a field trip?"

Mason slides the newspaper across the desk, and Willem glances at her perfect elliptical nostrils. He reads the headline she has circled for him. Why she wants to bother with some idiot who didn't have the sense to put his golf club down in a storm is beyond him. He slides the newspaper back across the desk to her and says, "I know you're into this weather stuff, but this might be reaching a bit."

"I've been following this guy for years. Do you know how many times he's been struck by lightning? Seven that I know about. When I first heard about him he'd been hit three times. I know you have trouble with math, so that's four hits in seven years. He's in the province now, so we can get on this guy. I need your help."

Willem leans back in his chair again, and allows himself a small smirk. He enjoys Mason's begging. Her asking him for help gives her a very attractive quality that he can't quite pin down. As he watches her, a wisp of black hair swings loose from her bun and licks the side of her nose. In a flash, he sees his own tongue along the side of her nose, tracing the gentle parabola that he's sure no one else has noticed…

"Willem?"

"Okay. We can fly to Toronto, and drive to Windsor. What is it? About an hour drive?"

"Three."

Finnigan sits on the riverbank at the southern tip of Canada, looking across at the city of Detroit. The dirt and grime of the Motor City slithers across the border on the heels of American teenagers who cross the border into Canada where they can legally drink and gamble two years sooner. Finnigan watches the imaginary line drawn on the Earth, where on one side some things are acceptable, and on the other side they are not. He wonders where in the river the line exists: if it is an infinitesimal filament, or the entire river itself.

The buildup of electrical energy in Finn's body some-times plays tricks on his mind. The river, for instance, seems stationary while the rest of the world rushes by, lapping at the edges of the water, while Finn tries to anchor himself but can't because somewhere, a lightning bolt is guiding him like a child tugging on a kite string.

A lightning bolt is a focal point of randomness, a compilation of uncertainties gathered into one concentrated burst, and for one instant, the exact result becomes certain; a buildup of electrical charge arcs from the sky to the ground. Finnigan can stand within this focal point and can become part of the collection of uncertainties and can, in fact, be the lens that converges the infinite possibilities into one. The force and energy of a lightning bolt can leave victims with severe burns and a scrambled nervous system. For some, amalgam fillings melt, watches fuse to the skin, pacemakers overload, clothing burns. For Finnigan, the electricity collects in his brain like a battery, leaving the rest of his body unaffected. He likes to take the strike either full in the chest or on top of his head. Two or three times the orientation of the bolt has been off, hitting him where he's not expecting it. In the back is the worst, because it leaves him sore for days. In the hours following a strike, even into the next morning, Finnigan's senses become finely tuned, especially his sense of touch. He runs his hands over the smooth rocks at his sides as bits of dust nestle into the grooves of his fingertips.

Another side effect of the lightning charge is his rampant paranoia. Acutely aware of everyone around him, Finnigan's mind overloads with information, information that only he is aware of, and to Finnigan this knowledge has a purpose. If the lonely teenager throwing rocks into the river a few hundred metres away, for example, were aware that Finnigan knew exactly what he was going to do tomorrow, he might throw those rocks at Finnigan instead. Knowledge, Finnigan has come to discover, brings danger.

A seagull trots along the edge of the river, searching the bits of garbage for something edible. The bird stands before Finnigan, who watches it and feels its hunger. It approaches him and tilts its head sideways, as if making a silent inquiry.

"I'm sorry," Finnigan says, "but it's your nature. You don't know what glass is." The bird hops around some more, then takes off in the direction of downtown Windsor. Finnigan doesn't look up when the bird flies into a low glass building, fooled by the reflection of the city on the other side.

Across town, Finnigan steps into his apartment. His phone just stopped ringing, probably the foreman wondering why he hasn't shown up for work this morning, or perhaps he read the paper today, and is calling to see if he will be in tomorrow.

Finnigan keeps very little furniture, and never buys a television. He grabs a canvas backpack from the closet and stuffs what few clothes he has into it. His watch has stopped at 11:32, and he throws it in the garbage. After he has collected everything, he leaves the apartment and does not bother to lock the door.

He buys a ticket for the six o'clock train to Toronto and sits in the station, watching people come and go. A man gets off the train with his much younger girlfriend who will win two thousand dollars tonight at the casino. Later, she will get extremely drunk and have sex with two young men up from Detroit for the night. They will take her money and leave her crying in the hotel, and she will be stuck because her older boyfriend will already be on the train home.

A young girl who has strayed from her parents crawls up to the seat next to Finnigan. She looks at Finn with the same eyes the seagull used earlier. He smiles and wags his fingers at her, and she smiles back. She takes out a toy truck that she will lose when she leaves the train station with her mother. Finnigan tucks a ten-dollar bill into the brim of the girl's pink hat, which her mother will find and use to buy the child a doll to replace her lost truck.

Finnigan leaves Windsor at six o'clock, roughly the same time Eric Able arrives at the apartment building where Finnigan Heller no longer lives.

Eric Able finds the door to Heller's apartment unlocked, and the room empty. The small apartment looks just as it should: not lived in. Finnigan must have used the counters for eating, because there is no table. A dusty old couch is the only piece of furniture. The cupboards are empty except for one plate, one bowl, and one mug. The pantry contains only a single, stale-looking tea bag.

On the bedroom floor is a mattress, a pillow and a

threadbare blanket—no sheets. Eric Able crouches next to the mattress, his nose checking the aroma left by its occupant, a smell of ozone and pine trees. He knew he would find nothing in the apartment, that Finnigan would be long gone, but it would be stupid not to check. All that's left is to figure out where he went. Heller has never left Canada, so south is definitely out of the question. That leaves only north, but where? Would he stop as near as London, or go all the way to Toronto?

A few beads of sweat trickle through his short hair and run down the sides of his face. Canada is a large country, and Eric Able is familiar with it only on maps. He has memorized aerial views of every major city in the country, but the dispersed nature of Canadian cities means that even if he is able to track Heller to the right city, it may take a long time to pinpoint him.

Pages of the file turn over in Eric Able's head. Finnigan Heller has never lived in the same place twice. He rarely even passes through cities he's lived in. He stays away from the smallest towns and the largest cities like Toronto, Montreal and Vancouver.

Eric Able journeys to the casino, placed close to the river, so that at night, people in Detroit can see the lights and feel the lure of the cheap Canadian dollar. Not an impressive casino, but odds are odds, and blackjack is blackjack, played with the same fifty-two-card deck everywhere in the world.

Able chooses a blackjack table with a lone player, a balding, greasy-looking man. The man is losing money with professional efficiency, and before long Eric Able is up six hundred dollars.

The greasy man has sixteen showing and says, "Hit me."

"The gentleman gets a nine. Bust."

"Goddamn it."

Eric Able says, "Hit me."

"The gentleman receives a four. Twenty-one, and a winner."

Eric Able collects another fifty dollars.

"Good Christ," the greasy man says. "You've only lost one hand. How do you do that?"

Eric Able ignores him and plays another hand.

"Alright, I'll show you how to play some blackjack. Hit me," says greasy.

"The gentleman already has nineteen showing."

"That's right, they call it gambling for a reason. Hit me."

"The gentleman receives a four. Bust."

"Hit me," says Eric Able.

"The gentleman receives an ace. Blackjack."

The greasy man loses his cool and puts a meaty hand on Eric Able's shoulder. "Now listen here, friend. You've won a little too much money here for my taste. You tell me how you're doing that!"

Eric Able swivels his head to look at the man, and stares at him with dead eyes. The hand falls from his shoulder. "Advanced number theory."

"Say what?"

"I'm sorry," Eric Able says, "but it's your nature. You just don't understand blackjack."

"Are you saying I'm stupid?"

"Aren't you?"

The greasy man is no longer able to hold the stare and scampers off. Eric Able wins several more hands of blackjack before three large men in red blazers approach the table. One of the men puts his hand on the back of Eric Able's neck.

"Excuse me, sir," he says. "We don't allow card counters in this casino. I'm afraid you're going to have to leave."

"How much does he have?" one of them asks the dealer.

"A little over nine hundred."

"Okay, sir. Let's go." One of the men collects the chips while the other two clasp Eric Able around the elbows and lead him to the front doors. Eric Able looks around the casino, watching hundreds of human beings living on chance, not a single one of them knowing if the next minute will bring shame or fortune. Oblivious to the security guards escorting him out, he fixes on a young woman dressed in a tight purple dress and wearing too much mascara playing a slot machine with an older man in a tweed suit. Eric Able can see the anticipation in the woman's eyes as she pulls the arm of the machine. A few seconds later, five sevens appear on the screen; she has just won two thousand dollars. She screams, hugs the older man next to her, and orders two glasses of champagne.

At the front doors, the guards release Eric Able, and the third guard comes up with a handful of Canadian dollar bills. "Alright sir, there's your money. Next time you don't want to be a card counter, got it?"

"But there are only fifty-two. How can't you?"

In his hotel room, Eric Able sits on the edge of his bed with the lights off. He knows where Finnigan Heller is going, just like he knows when the next card in the deck is going to give him twenty-one, he just has to figure it out. Finnigan Heller and Eric Able have a connection, even though they've never met, even though Heller has no knowledge of Eric Able's existence. They will cross paths. They already have crossed, it's just that that moment in time has yet to happen. Heller will go to Toronto, but he will not stay there.

On the television rests the file folder labelled with Heller's name. It's closed: Eric Able does not want the distraction, the indulgence of the past. He needs new information.

Able turns on the television and switches to the weather channel. Clear and sunny for the next two days in Windsor. Partly cloudy and a possibility of light showers for some areas of Toronto. A twenty percent chance of thundershowers in areas west of Toronto.

Does he follow the weather or does the weather follow him?

Finnigan Heller is going west.

"Listen, I've never heard of a guy named Finnigan Heller, okay? You must have the wrong place. There's lots of construction in the city. Maybe you got it wrong."

Mason and Willem stand in the mud in the unfinished foundation of a soon-to-be-erected shopping mall. The foreman, while polite, is proving to be difficult.

"His landlady specifically said here, Mr. Lipking. Now if you don't know the names of all your workers, maybe you could get us a list, and we'll look ourselves," Mason says.

"Lady, we're real busy here, so I don't have time to get a list for you. Sorry, but you're out of luck."

Willem puffs his chest out and says, "That's fine. Maybe we'll just make a call to the labour board, and they can help us out."

The foreman squints in the sun at Clyde Willem. "Who did you say you were?"

"RCMP. We need to ask Mr. Heller some questions. If you help us out, we can look the other way on any labour laws that you might be overlooking."

"Alright, alright. He didn't show up to work yesterday, and he's not answering his phone. I was paying the guy under the table, that's all. Some of the guys said he was in the hospital, something about getting hit by lightning. Is that what this is about? Am I in trouble here?"

"Thank you, Mr. Lipking."

Willem sits in the driver's seat of their rental sedan. "Sorry Mason, looks like he took off. So much for your red herring."

"Wild goose."

"What? Listen, let's get something to eat, spend the night, and get back to Ottawa tomorrow."

"He could have asked to see your badge. Where would we be then?"

"In the same place we are now. Nowhere. What was I going to say? We're with the Secret Police? That would have given him a laugh."

"He's so close, I know it. He can't be far."

"We don't have forever, Mason."

"Damn it." Mason leans back in her seat with her eyes closed. She massages the bridge of her nose up to where it meets her brow. Willem watches and licks his lips unconsciously. That's when he sees it. A small imperfection in the skin, almost like a mole, but very faint, as if under the skin. The sun bounces off her nose from the other side, creating a white aura around it. The mole is only visible in this perfect light. Willem shifts in his seat.

"We're going back to the hotel."

Willem yells through the door to Mason's hotel room. "I thought we were getting something to eat?" The latch clicks, and Mason opens the door.

"What?"

26

"Dinner."

"No time for that. Come here, I want to show you something." Mason leads Willem to the table in the room, where the file on Finnigan Heller is laid out. "Maybe he follows the weather. He could be a human lightning detector, and just not know it. He might be compelled to follow without realizing why."

"And if we follow the weather, we'll find him?"

"That's a possibility."

"Mason, do you have any idea how many thundershowers there are in this country right now? He can't follow them all."

"No, but he might get to the nearest one. Turn on the television."

Willem turns on the TV and finds the weather channel. Chance of thundershowers in areas west of Toronto. "This is a pretty thin theory you have. I don't know if it's enough to justify…"

"I know. But it's all we've got."

"No, it's all *you've* got, Mason."

"Fair enough. But Willem, I need your help. Can we please just give it a bit more time?"

"Fine. Now let's go get something to eat."

"We'll get it to go. If Heller left yesterday, we need to get moving."

On the highway, Willem drives the rental while Mason reads the file. Willem stuffs stick after stick of chewing gum in his mouth to kill the hamburger and french fry breath. He can taste the processed cheese and oil between his teeth, rotting his breath. All he can imagine when he looks at Mason's nose is his own tongue coated with smelly mustard and pickles. At the moment, he has six sticks of gum wadded up in his mouth, and he is unable to speak around them.

Mason moves her flashlight over the documents in the file. Most of the information is weather related; weather patterns in places with confirmed lightning strikes, a failed project to predict Heller's movements, statistical information on lightning, rainwater deposit estimates, and so on. At this moment however, Mason is reading over the limited biographical information on Finnigan Heller. Born December 14, 1975 in Fairmont, British Columbia. High School Diploma, Sir Winston Churchill High, Calgary, Alberta, 1993. No university education. Beyond that, there is very little information. A few blurry photographs and newspaper clippings. He would be the most unremarkable man, except that he seems to be an aberration of nature. At the hospital in Windsor, they said that not only was Heller lucky to be alive, but that it was miraculous that he wasn't seriously injured. Mason handles an enlarged print of Heller's high school photo. He wasn't smiling, and his eyes weren't looking into the camera, but away, as if he was looking at something else. His gaze wasn't absent, like he was smoking pot with his buddies on picture day; he was looking at something specific, Mason is certain of it.

Finnigan looks out the window on a bus bound for Calgary. In ten years he has not been back to that city, and he won't stay long. After three days in Calgary he will leave, but he doesn't know where to.

The man sitting next to him on the bus will have sex with a prostitute in Regina tomorrow night, and she will steal his credit card to buy herself a new television, groceries, and gasoline for her car. The man won't realize his card is missing for several days, and because he has no theft insurance, all of the bills will fall squarely on him. The interest alone will throw his tight monthly budget into the red, and his sister, who rents her basement suite to him, won't get the money he owes her.

The man, wearing jeans and a fleece jacket, pats his thighs and looks at Finnigan out of the corner of his eye. Silent, Finn looks out the window, watching the darkness stream by. The man next to Finnigan tries to make eye contact, but Finnigan seems entranced by the dark highway. Finally the man ventures, "So. What do you do?"

Finnigan wrenches his eyes from the silent road outside and looks at his companion, who seems trapped by nervous boredom. "Nothing."

"No no, not what *did* you do. What do you do. I mean for work."

"I heard you correctly. Nothing. How do you define your life?"

"Well, I'm a writer actually. I work mostly as a journalist. Have a job interview in Regina. Not exactly New York, but I'll take it. Where you heading?

"Calgary."

"Yeah? Family out there?"

"No."

"Just sightseeing, or what?"

"Are there sights in Calgary?"

"Mountains, I suppose. Skiing in the winter, hell I don't know. You must have some reason for going to Calgary."

"Yes, I do."

"This is like an interrogation. I'm just making conversation, buddy. I'm Ernest. Ernest Cook." Ernest Cook puts his hand out.

"Finnigan Heller. You can call me Finn." Finn shakes his hand, then stares out the window again.

"You were telling me why you're going to Calgary."

"I don't know."

"You just said you have a reason."

"Yes."

"What is it?"

"Do you know why the sky is blue, and why it turns orange when the sun sets?"

"What? No."

"Do you accept that there is a reason?"

"Sure."

"The sky does not know why it turns orange when the sun sets."

"Is that some kind of Zen stuff?"

"It's possible."

Ernest Cook smiles. "I like your style. I'm going to write an article about this bus trip. I don't know how I'm going to cram it in, maybe an opinion piece or something, but I'm definitely writing about this bus trip."

"No, you won't."

"Are you asking me not to write about you?"

"I'm not asking you anything. But you're not going to write an article on me, or this bus trip. When you disembark in Regina, you will forget about me."

"Hey, look. I'm just trying to be friendly."

Finnigan looks Ernest Cook in the eye and smiles warmly at him. "I know. Thank you." Finnigan searches for the best possible outcome among many, and says, "When you get off the bus, don't pay for the taxi in cash. Use your credit card." Ernest Cook, careless with his credit card, will not put the card back in his wallet, but will slip it into the back pocket of his jeans, where it will stay, forgotten, while he is out with the prostitute.

"What the hell are you going on about?"

"I just changed your life."

When Finnigan arrives, he takes the train to north Calgary where he checks into a hotel. In his room, he unplugs the television, makes certain all the blinds are shut, and lies

31

awake in the dark. In two days he will walk to Nose Hill Park, where the sun will shine despite heavy rainfall.

Raindrops start to pelt the window, and Finnigan sits up. Could his timing be off? He opens the sliding door to the balcony and stands in the drizzle. Off in the distance, sheet lightning. No, he's not late. The air doesn't have the right charge. Nature is only bluffing.

Calgary swallows up more land area than any other city in Canada. While in one part of the city the sky spits rain, another part sears in sunlight. Rolling hills and the Bow River ripple the landscape, giving Heller many places to hide. Eric Able arrives at the airport with no clue of how to proceed. He has no proof that Heller is in this city, but he knows that he is here somewhere. Heller is a drifter, and if Able cannot track him down within a day or two, he will drift once again.

Severe thundershowers are expected for the region today, so Heller could move on as soon as tonight. Eric Able is now closer to his life's work than he's ever been, and he is willing to lose his life before losing Heller.

In the map of Calgary in his mind, Able searches for the likeliest place Heller will go in a thundershower. A few golf courses dot the map, but the only people likely to get hit there are golfers who are too stupid to know when it's time to go inside. Lightning bolts can be unpredictable, but when you stick a metal pole up in the sky in the middle of a flat field with your shoes firmly planted in the ground, you're just asking for it.

But is that not what Heller's doing? Is he not asking for it? Which again brings up the question: is he following the weather or is the weather following him? Does Heller think that he just has incredible luck (good or bad), or does he really desire the lightning? Eric Able is convinced there is more, there must be.

Able scans his mental map of Calgary. He envisions an odd formation in the north part, like a fat lump, a tumour in the city. Nose Hill Park. This is where Finnigan Heller will go to be struck by lightning.

The pouring rain mars visibility, and the taxicab Eric Able sits in doesn't seem to be touching the road very much. Despite the driver's inability to keep the car grounded, he drives calmly with one hand, spending most of his time with one eye darting to the back seat so he can carry on a conversation.

The driver wears bifocals and has a tendency to squint his eyes every few seconds, making Eric Able wonder if he has something stuck in there, and if so, why he's piloting a vehicle in monsoon conditions. "That accent," says the driver, "that English, or what?"

"That's right."

"You in on business, or you just on vacation?"

"I can't imagine anyone coming to this city on vacation."

"Don't I know it. It's like some kind of weather vortex. One second it's sunny and hot, the next we're getting four feet of snow. No exaggeration. Good city for cab driving though. A lot of roads. Always someone coming or going, and in every direction. Sometimes I look in a car next to me and I see a guy, and I think, there's a guy I don't know and never will, and he has a whole life out there, with kids and a wife, wears a suit to work and goes to his house wherever, and has feelings and worries, and it's like there's a whole other world out there. You know what I mean?"

"No."

"Yeah, it's confusing. Hey, you sure you want to go to Nose Hill in this weather? It might not be safe up there."

"How much farther?"

"We're coming up on it now. You meeting someone up here?"

"Yes."

"I hope he has an umbrella. Here we are. Twenty-two fifty."

Eric Able stuffs twenty-five dollars into the driver's hand, not because he wants to leave a tip, but because he can't stand carrying those abysmal Canadian coins around in his pockets. As the driver pulls away, Able finds a path and climbs to the top of the hill. Smell and sound are the only senses he can use up here in the darkness. Heller will be invisible, and finding him will be almost impossible, so Able must wait until the bolt drops.

He tilts his head up to the sky and drinks in the rainwater. His fingers are spread out to the wind, and he hears thunder roll in from the west. But something about the air distresses him. Something is wrong with the smell.

Under his closed eyelids, he detects a flashing, almost like a strobe light. And someone is yelling. Opening his eyes, Eric Able sees a flashlight some distance away. Why would Heller bring a flashlight up here? Assuming that person *is* Heller.

A female voice yells two words that freeze him: Finnigan Heller. All this time Eric Able has been studying Heller—following him, analyzing weather patterns, questioning experts on the physics of lightning bolts—it has never occurred to him that someone else might be looking for him.

And for the first time in his search, Eric Able panics.

He slips towards the flashlight, shielded by the rain and the darkness, trying to move in behind the woman. She is only a few metres away, yelling Heller's name over and over again. Not only is someone else looking for Heller, but she beat him here. Able will not let her take him away.

As he gets closer, Eric sees there is a man with her. He's big, and not in an amateur bodybuilder way. Law enforcement, maybe even military. The woman is no threat physically, but he'll have to be wary of the man. Able gets behind the woman, brings his forearm around her throat and squeezes. The man tries to pry him off, but a kick to the groin solves that problem. Now it's just this woman, who has the audacity to speak Finnigan

Heller's name. How dare she come here! She sputters, and he loosens his grip just enough for her to take in a lungful of rain. That should finish her quickly, Able thinks, and he is so engrossed that he doesn't feel the first blow to the side of his head. The second strike catches him on the temple, and he sees spots. The third blow lands directly on the bridge of his nose, breaking it. The woman struggles free, and the man hits him between the legs. Able goes down, mud and grass filling his nostrils, and the two strangers disappear in the rain.

Eric Able is blinded. He can barely see, and the blood pumping out of his nose has robbed him of his sense of smell. Physical pain doesn't bother him, but the pain of having been beaten to his goal by unknown competitors almost makes him weep. He wants to lie in the grass and die, but the rain stops, and he sees the moon. No lightning.

Eric Able sits up, blood dripping from his face to his shirt, the second one ruined on this trip so far. He did not lose consciousness, and the thunder from a lightning bolt this close couldn't be missed. Heller is not out here, he was never out here. And now, he doesn't know what's worse, being beaten out here by that stupid man and woman, or being wrong about Heller's whereabouts when he felt so certain.

But he wasn't beaten out here. Heller was never here, so whoever those two were, they didn't get to him. Eric Able stands up and starts to walk down the hill. His objective is now much more urgent. They were probably following the weather, just as he was, meaning they must know at least as much about Heller as he does. They are all on the same curve now, Eric Able, Finnigan Heller, and the two strangers. Finding Heller may now mean finding them, and finding out what they want with Heller.

He should have known when he smelled the air. No ozone.

"Are you okay?" Willem has one hand on the wheel and another on Mason's back as she tries to cough the water out of her lungs. "Are you alright?"

"Yes," she manages, "just watch the fucking road!" She hacks and chokes, discharging a good deal of water and mucous from her nose. For the first time, Willem is turned off.

"Who was that guy? Was that Heller?"

Mason steadies her breathing. "He tried to kill me."

"Do you think it was Heller?"

"I don't know, I didn't see him. Did you see him?"

"No," Willem shakes his head. "He got me in the pills. All I saw was white spots. Good thing we had that umbrella. Hell, I don't even know what Heller looks like. I think I broke the asshole's nose, though."

"Could someone else be looking for him?"

"Someone sharing your bizarre obsession with this guy? I doubt it. It probably was Heller—he decided to have his way with you before he fried his brain under a lightning bolt for the thirtieth time. Goddamn perverts and their sick fetishes."

"Good thing I had a big strong man like you to come to the rescue."

"Make jokes if you like Mason, but if you had been out there alone, we wouldn't be having this conversation."

"Right. Okay, thanks then. Don't make a scene about it. It's not like we're engaged or anything."

"You're welcome."

Mason lies under the covers with the lights out while Willem sits in a chair and watches TV. Willem is a constant source of discomfort for Mason, but he did somehow manage to make himself useful today. Under normal circumstances, she never would have let him in her room with the lights out, but tonight she didn't feel like being alone. Even if an ape like Willem was her only company.

"Which of the following is an elementary particle?" the television announcer asks, "A: electron, B: positron, C: quark, or D: cation?"

"Quark, you dumb idiot," Willem barks at the screen.

"That's a tough one. I think it's a positron, 'cause I've never even heard of that before," says the contestant.

"Come on. It's a quark! There's no such thing as a quark, you dummy! They're just suckering you," Willem says.

"I think I'll go with 'B,' positron."

"You idiot! That's twenty thousand dollars you just flushed down the toilet," Willem informs the contestant.

Mason says, "Cation."

"Oh, sorry," the announcer says. "The correct answer is 'D,' cation."

"Bullshit. This show's no good. Hey Mason, there's no such thing as a quark, right?"

"Sorry, Willem. There is such a thing as a quark. It's an elementary particle."

Willem switches off the television and stands in the darkness. An artificial orange light seeps through the blinds, giving Willem's silhouette an odd halo. "Why're you after this guy, Mason?"

"What's a man like him like? What kind of thoughts go through your mind when that much electrical energy is surging through your brain?"

"Probably, 'I hope I'm wearing clean underwear,' would flash through your brain."

"He's never been burned, his nervous system's never been damaged. He can hold a job, he pays his rent. His landlady loved him, said he saved her cat. But he never stays in any one place for long. And no matter where he goes, the lightning is always there. He can't escape it."

"Maybe he doesn't want to. He might like it. He's a thrill-seeker."

Mason sits up in bed. "He's more than a thrill-seeker. He has a great big bull's eye on the top of his head, but I want to know if he wants it there, or if he *needs* it there."

"What if it's just dumb luck? He might just be the poor

sap who comes along to balance out those bastards who win the lottery four times. We should just go home."

"No."

"He tried to kill you."

"I don't think that was Heller. Someone else is looking for him."

Willem sighs and flops down on the edge of the bed. "Okay, that wasn't him. What do you want to do next?"

"I don't know. I'll look at the forecast tomorrow. There was no lightning on that hill tonight, was there?"

"Nope."

"And Heller wasn't there. Does he follow the weather, or does the weather follow him?" The question twists in her mind. It's not luck, it can't be. One strike is bad luck. Two strikes and you've won some kind of reverse lottery. Three strikes and the universe has your number. But seven? Seven that she knows about, and probably more, all without sustaining any injury.

"Hey, Mason?"

"Yeah?"

"I'm glad you're okay."

"You're not scoring tonight, Willem."

"Right."

Willem guzzles a glass of water back in his hotel room. He's still sore from the blow earlier, and he's not sure if he could have scored with Mason even if she wanted to. His quest to find her next to him in bed has turned into a dangerous game. Whoever that lunatic on the hill was, they will very likely run into him again if they keep on looking for Heller. If he has a busted nose when they find him, then Willem very much intends to give him a little more before they haul him off to the psycho ward. If he doesn't…

Willem contemplates for the first time the possibility that someone else really is looking for Heller. Someone ready to kill a woman he's never seen before. Willem keeps himself in good shape, and likes to think he's ready for anything, but he knows that law enforcement in this country is far from hazardous. The intelligence community is even less risky, considering that they don't have intelligence on anyone more important than the CEO of the Hudson's Bay Company.

So if someone deadly is looking for Heller, then he must be as important as Mason says. Willem slips into bed, and wonders if this Finnigan Heller guy realizes that someone almost got killed for him tonight. Two people for that matter, as Willem now realizes—as soon as that nut was finished with Mason, Willem would have been next.

When the rain stops, Finnigan wanders the city. His stomach is knotted from not having eaten in a few days. He finds a convenience store and picks up a few pastries and a hot chocolate. The clerk will go home at 4:30 a.m. to his girlfriend, who will tell him she is pregnant. Tomorrow, he will ask her to marry him, and she will say yes.

The moisture in the streets evaporates into Calgary's dry air. Plenty of rain, but only a bit of sheet lightning. Nothing on the ground was hit tonight, which is how it should be. The lightning won't come until the night after next, when the forecast calls for clear skies and twenty degrees.

Two cats fight over a piece of chicken in an alley. Finnigan watches them, listens to their cries and hisses. One cat is mostly grey and is missing half an ear, a street veteran. The other is lighter and younger, new to the scene. The seasoned cat knows it has the other cornered, and will let its guard down in a moment of false confidence. The younger cat will take advantage, scratching the older cat across the face. The injured cat will back off, and the new champion will trot away with the piece of discarded food.

Finnigan watches the scene play out, and after the younger cat leaves, Finnigan approaches the old veteran. This cat has no home to go to, and years of street life have made it lonely, although it doesn't know it. It lies on the wet gravel, heaving and bleeding from the three gouges in its face. Finnigan kneels down and holds a bit of pastry to the cat's mouth. It takes the pastry between its paws and nibbles away at it while Finnigan picks the cat up and carries it with him to sit against a garage door.

He takes a napkin he brought from the convenience store and wipes the blood from the cat's face.

"Hello there. I'm Finnigan." The cat meows. It is in pain, but the cuts will heal fine. Finnigan takes the cat back to the convenience store for some water to wash the dried blood from its fur.

"Hey, you can't bring that cat in here," the clerk says.

"He's a good cat. I just need water. He's hurt."

"Well, okay. But make it fast."

Finnigan takes the cat into the bathroom and cleans the cuts properly with water. He'll do just fine now. When they come out of the bathroom, a taxi driver is buying a cup of coffee. On the way to pick up his fare, the driver will swerve to avoid a man on the road, holding his nose and bleeding from his head. The taxi will hit a lamppost, and the driver will radio for an ambulance—not for himself, but for the man who by then has collapsed in the road. The street he will collapse on is near Nose Hill Park.

Finnigan follows the driver outside. "Pardon me, but do you already have a fare?"

"Yeah, I'm on my way there. Where you heading?"

"Nose Hill Park."

"You're in luck, I'm passing right by it. But sorry, no pets allowed."

"He's a good cat. I'll pay extra."

"Fine. I'm doubling the fare, though."

Finnigan and the cat climb into the car, and Finnigan makes sure he sits on the left, directly behind the driver.

"Funny weather, isn't it?" the driver asks.

"I'm used to it."

"Uh huh. What's the cat's name?"

Finnigan looks in the cat's eyes. "Ulysses."

"Ulysses? What kind of a name is that?"

"A good one. He's a good cat."

"Right." Under his breath, the driver says, "Fucking weirdo."

Finnigan observes that the cab is on the correct road, and tugs on his seatbelt buckle. It is secure. He looks at Ulysses and puts him on the floor of the cab. Finnigan sits calmly and says, "Hang on Ulysses," right as the driver sees an injured man stagger into the road. He swerves, just missing the man, and loses control on the slick pavement. The windows shatter as the right side of the car collapses against the lamppost.

Finnigan picks up an alarmed Ulysses and looks at the man who has fallen in the road. Finnigan thanks the driver and leaves twice the fare he saw on the meter before it broke in the crash, plus a twenty percent tip. Finnigan gets out of the cab, ignoring the driver's yelling as he radios for an ambulance.

The man in the street is bleeding from the nose as well as from gashes on the side of his head. The ambulance will arrive shortly, and the paramedics will bandage him up and take him to the hospital. He will sleep most of the night, and the hospital staff will not know what to do with him, because he isn't carrying any identification. He will solve their problem by disappearing the next morning.

Finnigan takes Ulysses with him up to Nose Hill Park.

No one else is in the park, and Finnigan wonders why a man would be staggering around up here getting bashed in the head. Had Finnigan ignored his instinct and come up here earlier tonight, he would have been here at the exact same time as that man, and whomever else may have been with him. Nose Hill Park is an odd place to be in the rain in the middle of the night.

Paranoids like Finnigan remain paranoid in spite of the absence of physical evidence—it only serves to reinforce how careful and thorough the people following them are. Finnigan now sees that the man following him is so good at following him that he's anticipated his whereabouts.

Finnigan is afraid.

II

ERIC ABLE LOOKS AT HIS REFLECTION in the hotel room mirror and sees a wide bandage across his nose and several stitches over his left temple. A bandage is taped to his head just above his ear, underneath which is a bald spot where someone shaved him to apply the stitches. In the other room, the television is tuned to the weather channel, which is promising clear skies for Calgary for the next three days.

Eric Able cannot breathe through his nose. He cannot smell. For him, the other night on the hill was failure. Heller was not up there, meaning Able was wrong when he was certain he was right. The appearance of the two strangers meant that the methods he used to find Heller were available to any common investigator. Instead of being creative, of using his intuition, of using his connection with Heller to track him down, he's watching the fucking weather channel. His life is at the mercy of cable TV.

He charges over to the television and puts his left foot through the screen, sending shards of glass all over the room as the vacuum tube implodes. He picks up his briefcase and leaves the hotel, stopping in a coffee shop for a doughnut before he goes to the airport.

Predicting the future is a calculation of probabilities. The more factors involved in a situation, the more difficult the prediction. That's why there's always a sixty percent chance of showers, never one hundred percent, because the weather is a combination of too many factors to keep a firm grip on. The fewer unknown variables involved in the equation, the better the chances of seeing the correct outcome.

Eric Able orders a coffee with cream and sugar, and a sour cream doughnut. He even smiles at the girl behind the counter. The smile looks more like a sneer with his small teeth and thin lips, more sinister than inviting.

He sits in a booth in the corner, coffee steaming. He doesn't chew the doughnut but sticks chunks in his mouth and waits for them to be moist enough so he can swallow them whole. As soon as the coffee has cooled, he swallows it in two gulps.

Either the future is uncertain, or it is set already, and everyone just plays out his or her predetermined parts. Eric Able believes in the latter; most people call it fate or destiny. Eric Able has no word for this belief; the universe simply exists, and time is merely an accident of perception. In his mind, he has already found Finnigan Heller, it's just that he has yet to experience that moment in time.

This belief does not exclude free will; just because it's already happened doesn't mean he didn't make it happen.

After six hours, the girl working behind the counter

gets off shift, and looks at the strange man who has been sitting perfectly still in the same booth for the entire day. He is breathing, and his eyes are blinking, but otherwise he looks dead. She tells the manager that he's been sitting there all day, and only bought one cup of coffee and one doughnut.

The manager, a plump man with wispy hair, approaches Eric Able and asks if he's okay. Eric Able does not hear him. Eric Able is calculating probabilities in his mind. He does not see the girl serving coffee, the little girl with her mother in the booth next to him, the manager of the shop peering into his glassy eyes. He sees equations and series of numbers. The Heisenberg Uncertainty Principle states that both the speed and the location of any particle in the universe cannot be known, because by measuring one quantity, the other quantity is altered. Just looking at something changes it. Until the past two days, Eric Able did not believe in the Uncertainty Principle. Lightning is drawn to a particular spot due to distance and potential electrical energy. The quantities must be exact or there will be no lightning. A bolt of lightning is a huge discharge of static electricity that has built up in the clouds, awaiting the proper conditions for release. In looking for Heller on the hill, Eric Able and the two strangers may have altered conditions on the ground just enough to curb a lightning strike in the area. And if Heller is drawn to lightning by some kind of premonition, then he would have known not to be there, maybe subconsciously. In looking for Heller, they may have altered where Heller would be.

He would have to look for Heller indirectly, find some way to follow him without changing the natural course of events. He would have to close in on Heller slowly, and from a distance, waiting until the bolt came down before finally closing in on him.

This theory allows for the possibility that Heller is still in Calgary, or at least was in Calgary two days ago. This theory also means that the two strangers may not be as bungling as Eric Able thought. But their search for Heller may push Heller away from the places he's supposed to go, leaving him much harder to track down. Finding Heller means simplifying the equation. Reducing the search to its barest elements. The strangers must be removed from the equation.

The manager of the coffee shop stops asking Eric Able if he is alright. He asks the girl to phone the police. He gets nose-to-nose with Eric Able, looking in his eyes for signs of life. When Eric Able gets up, he almost bashes the manager in the nose because he does not see him.

Tracking down the two strangers might be difficult, because he shares no connection with them like he does with Heller. He calls a taxi and finds another hotel instead of going to the airport.

Who would be following Heller? They could be private investigators hired by Heller's family, but Eric Able has never found any evidence that the man has a family. The man did have the build of someone professionally trained, but why would he be with a woman clearly not equipped to deal with a physical confrontation? Eric Able contemplates the possibility that the man is an intelligence agent, if there is such a thing in this country.

Eric Able checks into a new hotel. He does not assume the two strangers are intelligence agents, he knows it. He does not make assumptions, he calculates probabilities. Their empirical information about Heller will be no better than his own, meaning they are no closer to finding him than he is.

"Do you think he may have been out there that night?" Willem takes in the magnificent view of a back alley from the balcony of his room.

"I don't know. I didn't see anyone get hit by lightning."

"Maybe we scared him off before he had the chance."

"I suppose that's possible."

"What are you going to say to him when we find him?"

Mason has rehearsed a number of speeches for when she finds Heller, and has decided on none of them. "I'm wondering what he'll say to us."

"You think he knows we're looking for him?"

"No."

"What's the forecast?"

"Clear skies for at least three days. He's here, Willem."

"Fine, he's here. It's a big city. I don't think we're

going to come across the guy looking in a back alley. He's probably sleeping under some stairs or in a bus shelter somewhere. I remember this time a few years ago, we were looking for these bank robbery suspects. They stole around fifty thousand, so we were looking in expensive restaurants and hotels, because it was an amateur job, and amateurs love to flaunt, so we thought it was just a matter of time. A couple of weeks later, some uniforms bring in this vagrant because he was taking a leak in a public fountain. Turns out he fit the description of one of the suspects. We go in to question him, and sure enough, it's one of the guys. Turns out, his buddies double-crossed him, ripped him off, beat the hell out of him, and dumped him in the street. He had nowhere to go, so he slept outside for two weeks."

"Did you catch the other guys?"

"Nope."

"So what the hell are you talking about?"

"There was no way for us to know that his friends would rip him off, so there was no reason to look for a guy pissing in a fountain. We don't know anything about this Heller guy beside the fact that he's been zapped by lightning an inordinate number of times."

"You're saying we need to know more about him?"

"He used to live here, didn't he?"

"Yeah, he went to high school here."

"Alright then. You want to chase storm clouds, or do you really want to look for this guy?"

Sir Winston Churchill High School is a brown-brick build-ing with narrow windows, crowded on the north side with smoking teenagers. Inside, recently waxed linoleum floors reflect the cream-coloured cinderblock walls. Beside the administration office is the library, the outside walls of which are covered with yearbook photos of the past. Finnigan Heller is in the class of '93, right where he should be. Mason squints at the miniature version of the photograph in the file.

"There he is."

"Where?"

"Right there." Mason puts her finger on the photo.

"What's he looking at?"

"I don't know. Let's go find someone who remembers this guy."

The principal of the school directs them to Mrs. Harver, a chemistry and math teacher who has been at the school for twenty-two years.

Mrs. Harver stands six feet tall, with orange hair and large eyes. In the courtyard just off the cafeteria, she tells Willem and Mason about Finnigan Heller.

"Very absent-minded," she tells them. "I imagined that if he ever used his intellect, he would have been teach-ing the class to me."

"So he got good grades?" asks Mason.

"Quite the contrary. He barely graduated. Doesn't mean he wasn't smart. He was hit by lightning twice in the three years he spent here. Didn't miss a day of school because of it. Is...is he in trouble?"

"No," Willem assures her. "But we do need to find him. Is there anything you can tell us about him that could help us? Family, old friends maybe?"

"Friends? No, no."

"The other students made fun of him?"

"His...experiences with the weather could have made him the most popular boy in school if he'd wanted. Very abrasive, very different. He asked one boy in class why he wouldn't look both ways before crossing the street, and the next day that boy was hit by a car. Broke his left hip. That started stories, let me tell you."

Mason says, "Wait a minute. He told a boy that a car was going to hit him in the street?"

"No. Finnigan just asked him why he wouldn't look both ways."

"You said he was abrasive," Willem says. "Can you tell us how?"

"He got kicked out of more than a few classes. Told the social studies teacher, Mr. Baricco, that his wife wouldn't be sleeping around if he could finish the job himself. Right in the middle of class."

"What did you make of that?"

"Maybe Finn was sleeping with Mrs. Baricco," she replies.

"Did he ever say anything like that to you?" asks Mason.

"No. I left him alone, and he left me alone. I didn't care for the way he treated the other kids in class, but..."

"You let him anyway?"

"Miss Mason, teachers need to pick their battles. Some students are beyond help by the time we get to them. More than one teacher argued openly with him in class. Is that better for the other students than the occasional insult? I didn't think so."

"You didn't try to help him?"

"He was a job for a social worker and a psychiatrist, not a high school teacher. I was glad to see him go, and I'm not sorry I haven't seen him since."

"He certainly made an impression. Sounds like a fucking asshole to me."

Mason gazes out the window as Willem drives the car. She told Willem not to drive back to the hotel, but to just drive around while she thinks. A student who sleeps with the social studies teacher's wife should be a god to his classmates. Assuming it was true—more likely he was egging the teacher on, but a kid with nerve like that would at least be a lower deity. Willem's droning cuts into her thoughts.

"...and then he says to me, 'only two officer. I gave the rest to my dog.' Can you believe that?"

"What?"

"I said, 'Can you believe that?'"

"Willem, when I asked you to drive around so I could

55

think, I really meant, 'Drive around. So I can think.' Not, 'Tell me every story about all the idiots you pulled over when you were on traffic detail.'"

"You know what I do when I need to work out a problem, Mason?"

"Yes. You talk too much. Which is exactly why you don't work out very many problems. I'm a scientist. Scientists need quiet time. I'll let you know when I need you to beat someone up again."

"Why don't you tell me what you're thinking of, then."

"I'm thinking of what Heller said to his social studies teacher and to that kid who got hit by a car."

"So? He was feeding it to his teacher's wife and gave the kid some good advice he should have followed."

"You don't really think he was sleeping with the teacher's wife, do you?"

"No, but he was a high school kid. High school kids say things like that all the time. When I was fifteen…"

"Spare me the insight into your juvenile forays, Willem. What I find more interesting is what he said to the kid. Was that a common high school insult when you were fifteen?"

"No. Are you suggesting he ran the kid over?"

"Maybe he just knew."

"Knew what? It was probably a coincidence. You do know what that is, right?"

"This guy's been hit by lightning ten times. The word 'coincidence' never really crossed my mind."

"I thought it was seven."

"That we know about."

"I'm prepared to have this conversation with you when you come back down to earth."

Mason's cheeks flush with anger. In his peripheral vision, Willem finds the tiny mole on her nose and it looks like...why, yes, it's turning a shade of pink along with her cheeks. Her anger gives her face some much-needed colour.

Finnigan slept on some flattened cardboard boxes in an alley with the cat the past night. If someone knew enough to be at the park, they could surely find out about his hotel room. The question now is, should he avoid the park tonight, or does he go there anyway, knowing someone may be waiting for him?

In his life, Finnigan has never missed a meeting with a lightning bolt. Every bolt meant for him has found him, and he's not sure he could resist one, even if he wanted to. So Finnigan decides to go up to the park early, and watch for anyone who may be watching him. It is every paranoid's dream to turn the tables on his pursuer.

Dusk approaches as Finnigan arrives at Nose Hill Park. Ulysses calmly chews away on some beef jerky Finnigan brought for the trip. Finnigan finds the right spot he will need to be in later, then finds a good spot to watch that spot. A grove of trees fifty metres away is perfect, and gives Ulysses somewhere to climb around while they wait.

Finnigan settles himself on a log. The sky is still cloudless.

Without instinct, Eric Able might try to find out about Heller's past. Try to find someone who used to know him when he was a child. The two intelligence agents, identified now as Clyde Willem and Penelope Mason, did just that. They were at the high school, just as Eric Able predicted. He wasn't able to get close enough to hear the conversation with the teacher, nor did he care. He knows everything he needs to know about Finnigan Heller, and now he knows everything he needs to know about his adversaries.

Clyde Willem is indeed a former law enforcement officer, and Penelope Mason is a scientist of some kind. Eric Able has identified Mr. Willem as the only threat, as Mason does not carry herself with much physical confidence. Willem probably hasn't met with a serious physical challenge in years, but a little adrenaline in that frame of his will make him more than a match for Eric, if the two face off on even terms.

They drove around for hours before going back to the hotel. As he thought, they learned nothing at the school to help them find Heller, because there is nothing to learn about him. His psychology is unknowable, his mind operates on a level different from that of normal people. They have succeeded in leaving themselves in the open, where Eric Able can subtract them from the equation.

Willem follows the woman into the hotel; by the way he walks, Eric Able can see that he will try to get the woman to go to bed with him, which will make for an excellent opportunity to act against them.

From the lobby, he can see that their elevator has stopped on the third floor. Able waits fifteen minutes, then takes the elevator up after them. On the third floor, he walks softly past every door, putting his ear to the wood, listening. A businessman watching sitcoms, two teenagers having sex, a woman talking on the phone, and...ahhh. Willem demonstrating again that he's the man, and he's making the decisions. Shouldn't be long now.

"Mason, if we don't find Heller by tomorrow night, we're leaving. We can't stay out here forever."

"I know."

"We're pushing it as it is."

"I know. I'll think of something."

"That's what you said yesterday." Willem pours two glasses of bourbon from a flask in his suitcase and slides open the balcony door for some air. "Here," he says, "have a drink."

Mason takes the glass of bourbon and puts it away in one shot. "Ah. Thanks."

"Bourbon tends to be a sipping liquor, but whatever makes you comfortable. Another?"

"Okay."

Willem pours her another drink from the flask, putting in a little bit more than he normally would. This time she takes two gulps to finish the drink. "You're going to make yourself sick, Mason. You don't drink much, do you?"

"Nope. I think I'd like to start, though." She gestures to his flask. "I can see you're a professional."

"Only when I travel."

"I don't want to go back."

Willem steps closer to Mason. "We can stay here, then."

Mason feels his breath on her face. He lifts a finger and traces the bridge of her nose. "Willem..."

"It's alright. We're just having a drink."

"No, I..."

Willem leans in and brushes the tip of her nose with his lips. "Shh." He kisses her on the lips. Mason doesn't kiss back, but she doesn't pull away, and Willem takes it as an invitation. He tugs at the top button of her blouse.

"Christ! Willem, piss off! You're about as smooth as a brick wall, and you have the sense of one, too. I knew this whole trip for you was..."

She goes on, but Willem stops listening when he hears what sounds like a hand on the doorknob. He noticed it when he first moved in on her, but it quickly disappeared. Now it's back, and someone is listening.

"...demand a certain level of intelligence, and you sure as hell don't measure up. No, I won't be quiet; the whole place can listen, I don't..." But Willem is pointing frantically at the door, all concern for getting laid leaving his face. Mason realizes what he is gesturing about and falls silent. "Oh, shit," she whispers.

"Keep talking," he whispers back.

"What do you want me to say?"

"Uh, just make like we're, uh, like we're getting it on."

"What the fuck is that going to do?"

"I have an idea. Trust me."

The thought makes her ill, but she does her best. "Oh, Willem, yes, how did you know I like that? Oh, yes."

He shakes his head at her. "Jesus, make it believable."

"Alright, you swine! Get on your knees! I know you were wondering what these handcuffs were for. Shut up! I'm in charge here."

Willem stares dumbly at Mason, forgetting for a moment that they're in danger.

"Whatever you're doing, do it fast," she hisses, then, "That's right, put the blindfold on."

Willem shuffles to the door and looks out the peephole and sees a man with a wide bandage across his nose. "It's him," he mouths to Mason, and moves next to her and whispers, "Get the car keys, they're on the table." She makes for the keys, and Willem flips on the television and puts it on mute.

"What the hell are you doing? I don't think this is time for the weather channel."

"Just keep going, I need a few more seconds."

"Oh yes! You're more man than I thought you'd be. I'm not the timid scientist you thought I was, am I?"

Willem flips to an adult movie channel and cranks the volume up. "Okay, let's get out on the balcony and get moving. He'll figure it out pretty quickly."

Mason steps out onto the balcony with the lewd sounds of the movie receding behind her. She heaves herself over the railing, and dangles her feet to the balcony below. Willem follows, and as they make it to the street, Willem looks up at the balcony and sees the man staring down at them.

"Willem, let's go! Come on!" Then Mason looks up and sees him, each of them frozen in the instant, two paths narrowly avoiding intersection. Willem gives the man the finger, then he and Mason hop in the car and squeal out of the parking lot.

Willem leans on the gas, the speedometer inching to 120 km. "How did he find us?"

"I don't know. Did you get a good look at him?"

"Yeah. Didn't look like Heller, but the picture we have is ten years old. That was a nice performance, by the way. The blindfold was a nice touch."

"Yeah, my mom read stacks of Harlequin romances when I was growing up. You wouldn't believe the filth in those things. And what the hell did you think you were doing back there?"

"Uh, well, I…"

"If you ever try to get me drunk and screw me again, I'll…"

"Okay. Calm down."

Silence prevails for many minutes. Shreds of clouds are tufts of gold and red in the coming night. The sky has clouded over since they arrived at the hotel; not enough to block the sun but…

"Mason, you said the weather forecast said clear skies, didn't you?"

"Yeah, so?"

"At the risk of sounding stupid, the skies sure don't seem that clear to me. Especially over there." Willem points to the north, where a blanket of black cloud has rolled in.

"Maybe we got here early. That looks like one fierce cloud."

A great shaft of blue-white light arcs from the clouds, and for an instant, Heller's silhouette is visible at the base of the bolt before he is flung across the field at the top of Nose Hill Park. Mason and Willem are close enough to see that Heller is wearing sunglasses when he gets knocked off his feet.

Mason is the first to his side. "Jesus, are you alright? Can you hear me?"

"Yes," Finnigan says.

Willem crouches down beside Mason. "Wow, did you *see* that? That thing had his *name* on it. Is he alive?"

"Yeah, he's alive. You're Finnigan Heller, right?"

"That's right. No autographs, please." Heller takes his sunglasses off and looks at Mason. "You have a really pretty nose."

Willem gives Heller the once-over. Not too remarkable looking: brown hair, brown eyes, thin physique. His hands, splayed open against the dark sky, sport long, elegant fingers, and Willem thinks he sees steam rising from the man's fingertips. "We should get him to a hospital, Mason."

"No," says Heller. "No hospital."

"Mr. Heller," Mason says, "we have to get you out of here. Someone is looking for you."

"You mean, besides the two of you?"

"Yes. He's dangerous, and he probably knows we're here."

"You mean the guy with the busted nose?"

Willem says, "Wait a minute. You've seen him?"

Heller sits up. "Oh sure. He was passed out on the road the other night. Mean-looking bastard. What do you two want?"

And that is the question. The same question Willem has been asking Mason for the past few days, the same question Mason has been asking herself. "Mr. Heller, right now we want to get you the hell out of here."

"Okay. But don't forget the cat."

Finnigan Heller lies in the backseat while Willem gets as

far away as possible from Nose Hill Park. The cat is purring loudly on Finnigan's chest, and Mason is turned around in her seat, not believing that she has found him.

"Mr. Heller, do you need anything?"

"You can call me Finn. And no, I don't need anything. I get very tired after a strike. I just need sleep." Finnigan puts his sunglasses back on, but his eyes remain open. The bulky man will drive to Canmore, where the three of them will share a cheap motel room. Finn will fall asleep first. The man and the woman with the pretty nose will talk for hours, then the man will fall asleep and snore loudly. The woman will lie on the bed propped up on her elbow half the night, staring at Heller.

Paranoids believe that they must be very smart to be constantly outrunning their pursuers. It never crosses a paranoid's mind that his pursuer could be friendly. Finnigan is not afraid because he knows that these people mean no harm, but he is disturbed because he was unable to avoid them.

Clyde Willem extends his middle finger up at the balcony, then gets into the car with the woman. Eric Able can see that the man thinks he is in a Hollywood action movie from the way he tears out of the parking lot, leaving thick bands of rubber smoking on the pavement. Willem is mentally weak, but the woman...the woman surprises him.

The charade ceased to fool him when she told Willem to put the blindfold on. The handcuffs were believable, but Penelope Mason is someone who needs to see your eyes. Eric Able knows this, just as he knows they will reach Finnigan Heller first. Before, this would have crushed him, because it would have meant defeat. Now, it means that Heller will be easier to find, because Willem and Mason are easy to find.

Eric Able starts to kick the door in as soon as he hears the TV come on, but his legs aren't as strong as they used to be and Willem and Mason are long gone before the door comes crashing in.

The adult movie is progressing in typically ridiculous fashion, sending phony howls through the hotel. Someone in the next room is banging on the wall—*Keep it down, you goddamn pervert!*

When two hotel staff members in green jackets arrive to investigate a noise complaint, Eric Able feels a cool gust of air. If his nose had been in working order, he would have caught the distinctive odour of ozone. In the north sky, a lightning bolt surges from a charcoal cloud that wasn't there ten minutes earlier. The thunder reaches his ears at the same time one of the men puts his hand on Eric Able's shoulder. In three seconds, both men are down, clutching their throats.

At his own hotel an hour later, Eric Able orders an adult movie, and stares at it as if the television were showing nothing more than program listings. He sees a woman handcuffing a man, which makes him think of Penelope Mason. Her performance became transparent very quickly, but now Eric Able realizes that the woman is in control. The brute Willem is nothing more than a bodyguard smitten with his charge.

From his briefcase, Eric Able retrieves a deck of cards, and the file with his information on Heller. He takes the cards out of the box and sets them on the file. Then, after staring at the deck for several minutes, he picks up the cards and shuffles them quickly, like a professional, and deals a game of blackjack with three imaginary competitors and himself as the dealer. As the performers on-screen spank and moan and scream away, Eric Able imagines a place for Penelope Mason on the left, Clyde Willem on the right, and Finnigan Heller directly across.

Willem is too stupid to play the game, and stays at ten; Mason does well but loses, holding at seventeen; but Heller...Heller hits at twenty, because he knows the next card in the deck is an ace, and it's the only way to beat the dealer, who also has twenty.

Not even dumb luck is enough for Willem, and Mason is doing what smart amateurs do, playing the odds. Playing the odds will not win her hands when Eric Able and Finnigan Heller are playing the game, though. Heller wins most of the hands. He knows when to hit, when to stick, and when it's impossible for him to win. Eric Able can count cards all he wants; it's still just a calculation of probabilities. Heller is not counting cards; he doesn't need to. He knows when the next card is the Jack of Hearts, or the Three of Diamonds.

On the TV, the woman finishes the man off with some very creative acrobatics, and Eric Able switches it off. Willem will think that the quest is over, and will want to stuff Mason and Heller onto the first plane to Ottawa. Mason, of course, realizes that the quest has only begun, and will want to accompany Heller to the next strike. Heller won't care what the two of them do, as long as they stay out of his way.

However, now that Mason and Willem are indivisible constants in the equation, they will have an effect on the outcome, perhaps even on the course of Heller's journey. The woman may even be strong enough to push Heller in the direction she wants to go. Like any good scientist, she will want to understand the origin of the phenomenon. For her, the key to Heller is his genesis.

Eric Able opens the file and turns to the very back, a place where he doesn't often go. A lone newspaper clipping, yellowed and brittle, older than the rest, is tucked into the flap at the back of the folder. Most of the headline is obscured, but the visible words read "Six Schoolchildren Killed by Lightning, One—"

All of the articles, all the photos and analyses, all the research are useless bits of paper to him now. He will leave the past to the woman travelling with Heller; Able wants the future. He hurls the folder across the room, and tosses the deck of cards back into his briefcase.

Mason lies in bed, propped on her elbow, watching Finn sleep. Willem is on the floor with a small pillow and a thin blanket. The cat, Ulysses, sleeps at Finn's feet. This cheap room is the best they could do on short notice, as there are no vacancies in any of the more respectable hotels. As far as anyone can tell, their pursuer is far behind them.

"At least we're not paying by the hour," Willem offers.

"What?"

"I just mean it's not as seedy as one of those hourly rate places."

"I guess you'd be the expert," Mason says, laying her head on the pillow.

"I'm, uh, I'm sorry about before," Willem offers. He twists his fingers together and can feel beads of sweat forming in his armpits.

"What do you mean?"

"It's my nature. I just don't understand women."

"I'll try to forget about it. Stop bringing it up."

"Listen," Willem says, "we should get on the first possible flight back to Ottawa. We have what we came for, and we've been gone long enough as it is."

"We just found him. You want to leave already?"

"Mason, what else do you want? We found the guy already. Let's get him on a plane, and get him back home."

"I doubt very much that he'll be struck by lightning inside a laboratory. I want to be there the next time it happens. I want to know what he's feeling, what he's thinking."

"Sounds real scientific. I don't see you analyzing a whole lot of weather patterns."

"I just want to talk with him for a few days, that's all. Aren't you the least bit interested in what's going on in his mind right now?"

"I do want to ask him about his high school social studies teacher."

"Go to sleep, Willem."

After five minutes, he does, and snores loudly. Mason wonders where Finn will go next, but she is certain she will be with him when he gets there. Looking at him now, she sees nothing she expected. She'd been fantasizing that Finn would be an attractive, mysterious man. So far, she's found him to be only average looking, and slightly abrasive. He certainly looks like a drifter should; unshaven, messy hair, dirty fingernails. Far from filthy, but he definitely hasn't showered in at least two days.

But she *is* drawn to him. Something about him suggests a coming together of sorts. Like pieces of a puzzle falling together to hint at the larger picture. A convergence of forces is around him, of which lightning is only the most obvious one.

Finn's chest rises and falls in perfect rhythm. A man struck by lightning only a few hours before, and he looks like he's been tranquilized. His mangy companion is very attached to him, and aggressive to everyone else; he almost scratched Willem's eyes out when he tried to get him into the car.

For most of the night, Mason watches Finn. The excitement of the night before still has her heart beating fast, and Willem snores too loud for her to sleep anyway. She replays the scene over and over, the instant the lightning bolt came down to smite Finnigan Heller. He wasn't afraid, he wasn't anxious, he just stood there waiting, even had the clarity of mind to put on a pair of sunglasses to shield his eyes. And for all the stupid things Willem has said over the past week, he was right: "that thing had his name on it."

Now, however, Mason wonders if maybe it was the other way around, if Finn maybe had that bolt's number.

Finnigan Heller eats a Belgian waffle with strawberries, blueberries, and extra whipped cream. Every few minutes he comes up for a breath of air, a sip of hot chocolate, then dives back down into his breakfast. On a side plate sit three strips of bacon and four sausages. The sausages are for Ulysses, who was forced to wait in the car.

Mason and Willem watch Finn inhale his food over two cups of coffee and a few pieces of whole-wheat toast. Speaking to him is impossible, for every time either of them asks him a question, he shakes his head and mumbles around a mouthful of food.

"I was thinking," says Mason, "maybe we should take him farther west. Fairmont is only three hours away."

"Fairmont? What the hell is that?"

"It's a little resort town in the mountains. He was born there."

"Why do you want to take him there? He probably doesn't remember the place very well."

"He might have family out there. Invermere is right there, too. There's got to be someone in the area who knows about him." Mason and Willem are whispering as if Finn can't hear them across the table. His eyes follow their conversation, but he knows before they do what they will decide on.

"Mason, who cares? You want to study the lightning stuff, fine. But we're not out here to write the guy's biography. Follow him around for a few days, wait 'til he gets zapped again, take his temperature, and then let's get out of here. And don't forget that psycho following us, either. The sooner we're away from *him*," Willem points at Finnigan, "the sooner we'll be away from him."

Finnigan is now a new breed of paranoid: one with proof. The two people who have tracked him down are indeed government agents. Finn feels a bizarre sense of pleasure and satisfaction at this justification of his paranoia. What really puts a smile on his face is knowing that there is yet another man after him, one of obviously sinister intent, if these two harmless blunderers are to be believed.

Finnigan stabs the last strawberry with his fork, stuffs a strip of bacon on the end of it, swirls it around in some maple syrup, and eats it. "Okay," he says between bites, "now's about the time where you tell me what you want with me."

"Finn, how many times have you been struck by lightning?"

"Seventeen."

"Extraordinary. Can I ask you some questions?"

"Sure."

"We talked to a teacher you had in high school, Mrs. Harver, do you remember her...? Anyway, she told us a story about a classmate who was hit by a car. She said that the day before, you asked him why he didn't look both ways before he crossed the street. Do you remember why you said that?"

"Sure, I remember that. I asked him, because I wondered why he wouldn't look both ways before he decided to jaywalk across a busy street. I don't remember his name though. Stupid kid, popular with the ladies, you know the type." He glances at Willem. "I guess he thought the traffic lights didn't apply to him."

Willem asks, "You knew he would be hit?"

"Sure."

"How?"

Finnigan shrugs. "Difficult to explain. I see it like you see the coffee in your cup. You know that within the next five minutes, the coffee in that cup will be gone. You're not seeing the future, you just know the variables, and your mind puts together what will happen. You don't need to think about it, and neither do I. I just see further than most people."

73

"Come on," Willem says. "You see the future?"

Finn takes a sip of hot chocolate and wipes a bit of whipped cream from his lip. "When Einstein was working on special relativity, he deduced that the speed of light is constant in all reference frames, without any kind of experimental analysis. At the same time, a couple of guys were proving the same thing, by accident, without Einstein knowing about it. Later, when he was working on general relativity, he just wrote down the field equation almost out of nowhere, then disregarded it. Four years later, after learning new kinds of mathematics, after all kinds of thought experiments and derivations, he came up with the same field equation he wrote down out of nowhere four years earlier, apparently with no knowledge that he had repeated himself. Was Einstein seeing the future? Or did he just know, and not trust it?"

"Mason, I think this guy's nuts."

Eric Able rents a car and takes the highway west out of Calgary. Driving on the left side of the car on the right side of the road is disorienting. The resort town of Fairmont is only three hours away, and Eric Able suspects that the party of Finnigan Heller hasn't even left Calgary yet.

The Rocky Mountains jut out of the landscape, rippling the ground around them into soft foothills. He knows the way; he has seen this road a million times in his mind. Past the tacky tourist trap towns of Canmore and Banff, into the thin, winding passageways between mountains.

On his left is a patch of forest recently ravaged by fire. Charred skeletons of trees poke up out of the ash not yet washed away by the rain. After a dry summer, an errant lightning bolt could turn countless square kilometres into an inferno, leaving nothing but a convenient perch for a passing bird.

Eric Able looks at the cloudless sky and his mind returns to the previous night. No doubt that lightning bolt he saw found Finnigan Heller. Those black clouds rolled in from nowhere, like they materialized just for Heller's benefit, at his will, even. Clear skies were reported for the entire area. Weather reports aren't always to be believed, but the shaky state of weather in this country surprises him. Here, a mass of dark clouds can roll in, hover for an hour, and then vanish as if they were never there. Rain can pour down while the sun shines away. And one man is at the centre of it all. What kind of chaos surrounds Finnigan Heller that he should be blessed with such a gift?

A gift that Eric Able needs to understand, needs to grasp, so that he might possess it himself.

Eric Able scratches the scar under his shirt. He received the injury many years before, and it tends to itch in higher altitudes. It runs across his spine, around his ribs on his right side, and stops at his hip. The doctors were unable to graft the skin properly, and the scar is a mangled, twisted mass of pink and white skin.

When Finnigan Heller is struck by lightning, he does not burn.

III

WHEN FINNIGAN HELLER DREAMS, he is always falling. He never jumps or lands, the dream starts mid-fall. Every time he has this dream, he is at another point in the fall, sometimes higher, sometimes lower. He doesn't feel vertigo or weightlessness, just a light breeze on his face to let him know he's on his way down.

In his dream, the sky is clear and blue, the sun bright and gold. He can see the ground, but it is too far away still for him to see any details. No sound but the wind, no sight but the sky.

Finnigan wakes in the backseat of the car to Ulysses licking his face. Outside he sees mountains. "Are we there yet?"

"We're about halfway," Mason says.

"Right. Hey, big man, keep your eyes peeled for a restaurant on the left side of the highway in about half an hour. They have really good chicken. On second thought, don't bother, you're not going to stop anyway. Oh, and you're going to have to take a leak soon, so you should start watching for a good place to stop."

Willem tightens his hands on the steering wheel. "I thought you couldn't see my future."

"See your future?" Finnigan chuckles. "Who said anything about seeing your future? You're just predictable." Heller has been napping in the backseat since they left Canmore, only to wake up every now and then to tease Willem before he goes back to sleep.

"Mason," hisses Willem. "If this guy doesn't shut up, I'm going to pull the car over and boot him into the ditch."

"Just relax, Willem. Ignore him. Finn?" Mason turns around in her seat and touches Finnigan's hand. "Is the other man waiting for us there? The man with the broken nose?"

"Hmm? Oh." Finnigan lifts Ulysses off his chest and sits up. "I don't know. From your story, he was able to find you before, so I imagine he'll find you again."

"Can't you, you know, see it?"

"No. I can see what people will do only when they don't know it. Once they know, they can change it, and then it's uncertain."

This news unsettles Mason. She always thought that when she found Finnigan, she would know what would come next. Now she sits with a man who can see ahead, and all of them are as uncertain as ever.

"Can I ask you about the lightning?" Mason ventures.

"I don't want to talk about lightning."

"The weather, then. Do you predict the weather?"

"No one predicts the weather. Meteorologists study numbers, and calculate probabilities. I can't see it any better than they can."

"Yes, I've studied the weather a great deal. That's why you interest me."

"That's not why I interest you."

At first, Mason thinks this is another one of his little jokes, but his tone suggests otherwise.

"Then why do you interest me?" she asks.

"That's the question, isn't it? And I can't say I know why. But never mind that...you were asking about the weather?"

"Do you follow the weather, or does it follow you?"

"Religious people often invoke the chicken-and-egg paradox to refute the evolutionary theory. No apparent answer exists, because one needs the other. The easy answer is that God made one of the two first, and that's that."

"Are you saying God throws lightning bolts at you?"

"God's gone AWOL, I think. Listen. When they're making coins at the mint, do they make heads before tails, or tails before heads?"

"I don't..."

"Neither. In three dimensions, you can't make one side to a coin, you have to make the whole coin. Each side needs the other in order to exist at all. Neither side came before the other, they came at the same time. This is the solution to the chicken-and-egg paradox. Everyone is so caught up in which came first, that they exclude the obvious answer. They came together."

Mason opens her mouth to speak, but makes no sound because she has nothing to say. Ulysses sits under

79

the rear window, his mutilated ear brushing the glass. His head swivels back and forth, like he is focussing on some static object beside the road, watching it until it vanishes from sight, then finding a new object and repeating the procedure.

"I don't think Ulysses likes cars," Finn says.

"Can you read his mind, too?" Willem jabs.

"No. His claws are digging into the seat though. He's holding on for dear life."

Willem pumps gas while Mason uses the washroom and Finnigan buys some chocolate bars. The man working the counter will fall asleep in a few hours, while taking his break in the back room. When he wakes up, he will find twenty-two dollars on the counter with a note telling him that the money was for sixteen dollars worth of gas, and about five-fifty in candy and snacks, and not to worry about the change.

Finnigan pays for his chocolate bars and throws a chunk through the open car window for Ulysses. Looking at the clouds, Finnigan can see an elephant, a starfish, and a large blob that looks like cotton candy. Rain is a possibility for the evening, but definitely no lightning for six days.

"Six days," Finn says to Willem.

"What?"

"In six days, I'll get hit by lightning again, and maybe then you can convince her to go home. On the other hand, she could fall madly in love with me, and you'll be flying solo."

"Your teacher was right," Willem says. "You are one fucking asshole."

"Sorry to disappoint you, big man. What did you expect?"

"Something to justify this whole trip. Mason even had me going for a while that there might actually be something to you."

Finnigan seems to think about this for a few minutes as he chews away on his chocolate bar. Finally, he puts his hand on Willem's big shoulder and says, "Don't worry about it, Willem. The universe is bigger than everyone. Even you." Finnigan smiles. "I've been hit by lightning seventeen times. There has to be something to that, don't you think?"

Mason comes out of the bathroom and sees Finn with his hand on Willem's shoulder. As she approaches, Willem finishes pumping gas, and brushes past her to pay.

"What were you talking about?" Mason leans on the car next to Finn.

"Oh, you know. Chicks, cars. The usual stuff."

"Do you have any family out here, Finn?"

"Maybe. I'm sure I'm related to someone somewhere around here."

"Do you know when...when the next one will hit?"

"Lightning bolt you mean? Yeah, about six days or so. After that, your big friend there will probably want to go home."

"Yeah. Poor Willem, he has no imagination." She tosses her hair over her shoulder so she can see Willem through the glass wall of the gas station. He's wandering the aisles, filling his arms with potato chips and other junk food. A bit of yellow sunlight catches her nose just right, and Finnigan sees the tiny mole that looks like it's under the skin.

"When did you first hear about me? I'm usually pretty good at keeping myself out of the papers."

"Do you do that because you're worried people will follow you?"

"Yeah. It was going well too, until the two of you showed up."

"We were studying abnormal weather effects at the time, and you certainly qualified, so we started a file on you. Your name just came up in the course of research. Random chance. Fate, maybe."

"Sorry. No such thing."

Mason tackles the last leg of the trip, while Willem munches potato chips in the passenger seat. Ulysses has calmed down a bit, and sits now in Finn's lap. The three-hour drive through the mountains has taken nearly six, as Finnigan has them stopping every time he sees a bear or a deer or a gas station. Wildlife is not Willem's concern, and he will snap if Finnigan asks them to stop one more time before they get to Fairmont.

"Big man, how many times would you need to stop for gas on a trip like this if you started in Calgary with a full tank?"

"Is that some kind of math problem or something?"

"No, no, I'm serious. Would you need to stop for gas over three hundred kilometres if you had a full tank?"

"Depends on the car, but no, you'd make it on a full tank, I'm pretty sure. Why?"

Finnigan says, "I've been looking at everyone we meet at every station we've stopped at. None of them will come into contact with the man chasing us. That could mean nothing, but it could mean he's figured out where we're going, and he's beat us there. Or maybe you lost him."

"That's the smartest thing you've said all day," Willem says.

"Are you jealous?"

"Finn," Mason says before Willem has the chance to bark back, "if he's waiting for us, maybe we should turn around. Call me crazy, but I don't think he's friendly."

"I don't know, all of a sudden I have an urge to introduce the two," says Willem. "Maybe he'll stop trying to kill us. He's looking for you, Heller. Not us."

"He's trying to find me, but he's *looking* for you. To him, I'm unpredictable, like the weather. You two went through the standard search machine: found out about my childhood, where I was born, what I like to eat. Since the two of you found me before he did, he just has to follow your footsteps, which he's been doing all along. You see, it wasn't me he was looking for at your hotel room, it was you two. By the way, the story of that porno stunt really puts a smile on my face."

"He knows we're linked now," Mason says.

Finn nods. Willem says, "Thanks a lot, Heller."

"I didn't invite you out here. And I'm not here to fulfill some kind of calling either one of you might have. I'm just a guy. You can forget everything you know about fate, nature, life, and especially about me."

Around 6 p.m. Mason pulls off the highway into the town of Invermere, about a half-hour from Fairmont. Invermere is a lakeside community, but considerably larger than Fairmont, providing the surrounding areas with police and hospital services. The main draw of the town is the excellent windsurfing and fishing. Like many of the places Finnigan finds himself in, it's filled with people coming and going, very rarely with people staying.

"What are you doing? We're almost there," Willem says.

"Whether that man is waiting for us or not, we have six days before Finnigan needs to be in Fairmont. We should keep out of sight, and that'll be easier here. Fairmont isn't a bustling urban centre, you know."

"I don't see any high-rises out here either."

"I'll work on my tan then," she says.

Eric Able sits in the natural hot springs at Fairmont. For a few hours, he loses himself in the hot water and steam, and finds he is enjoying himself watching the mountains.

Back home, there are no mountains like this. Young and sharp, the Rocky Mountains pulse with vibrancy and life.

And the water! Eric Able loves the water. On the outside, Eric Able sits stoically, unmoving, but inside he is a child, splashing and swimming and squirting water out from between the slight gap in his front teeth.

Eric Able thinks then of Heller, and wonders how often swimming pools like this are struck by lightning. Spring water, filled with minerals, would conduct electricity very well. Dozens of people, flash-fried to perfection, leaving a smoking, steaming mass of cooked flesh. All except for Finnigan Heller, who would walk out of the pool, towel himself off and say, "Nothing like a nice dip."

The heat starts to make Eric Able's mind swim, so he gets out of the hot pool, and wades into the adjacent cold one. A little girl sitting in the water with her father points at Eric Able's scars in full view and asks, "Daddy, what happened to that man?"

"Isabel, *shush!*"

The cold water brings Able back to reality. He suspects that the woman, Penelope Mason, has checked the trio into a hotel in Invermere in a vain attempt to stay out of sight. This is just fine. He doesn't need to watch the weather channel anymore.

In the shallow end of the pool, a group of four children are playing, splashing around, playing tag in the water, and seeing who can hold his or her breath the longest. Their parents, practising modern parenting, are nowhere to be found. Eric Able is sitting in the corner, not far from the playing children, the water just reaching his chin. Pretending to make it look like an accident, one of the children splashes Eric Able in the face. Proud of himself for about three seconds, the child is frightened when the strange man doesn't move, or even close his eyes against the water. He sits and stares. Before he knows why, Eric Able splashes the child back.

This incites retaliation, and soon the children are caught in a war with the strange man. The game seems to be who can get the most water on the adult, and they all work together to bring Eric Able down. His head sinks under the water, and he is defeated.

After much laughter, they wonder why the man stays under the water. None of them really understands what it means to drown, but they know that air is very important. Just as they stop giggling, Eric Able peeks out of the water and shoots a thin stream from between his front teeth, right between the eyes of the boy who originally splashed him. There is another round of splashing until the careless parents return and pull their squealing children from the pool, berating them for misbehaving.

One man yanks his son's arm and says, "You know better than that! You apologize to that man, right now!"

The boy turns to Able and squeaks, "Sorry, Mister."

Eric Able smiles at him.

Lightning tends to strike the highest point available, taking the path of least resistance to the ground. The driving force behind a lightning bolt is electricity itself. Like gravity, electrical attraction is a fundamental characteristic of the universe. Negative charge attracts positive charge; neither charge can avoid the other because nature does not allow it. Heller "knows" where the lightning will come down just as anyone who jumps from a roof "knows" he will fall. No other outcome is possible. Eric Able does not need to look for Heller any longer, because Heller will come to him. Being built at the base of a mountain, Fairmont has many places ideal for lightning, all of them accessible to Heller without the help of Eric Able. There's only one option left for Able: the only way to know for sure where Finnigan Heller will be when the lightning comes down is to ask him.

"I was born in a parking lot," Finn tells Mason and Willem. "My mother went into premature labour in the Fairmont Hot Springs parking lot after a quick swim. By the time the ambulance got there, I was out, and she was dead."

The three of them sit on the beach at dusk, Finnigan assuring them that it's safe; no one Finn has seen yet will see the man with the broken nose for at least a day or two. Mason has managed to curb the bickering between the two men, forcing them to keep a civil tone.

"Sad story," Willem offers, almost genuinely.

"Yeah, I should be on TV."

"Quiet," Mason hisses. "Enjoy the sunset."

"You don't have a metal plate in your head, do you?"

"Willem!"

"No, I'm serious. There has to be some good reason why you keep getting scorched. Maybe God's trying to tell you something."

Finnigan speaks, but not to acknowledge Willem's joke. "A few hundred years ago, before anyone really knew what lightning was, do you know how they explained it?"

"How?"

"Same way they explained everything else. It was God's wrath. You stubbed your toe? I guess you shouldn't have missed church on Sunday. You burnt the roast? Maybe you shouldn't have looked at the new farmhand's under-garment area. Now guess what lightning struck more than anything else? Church steeples. Looks like the Almighty's pissed off again, that's why he burned all those faithful churchfolk alive while they were busy worshipping him. Guess we should pray harder next time." Dipping below the horizon, the failing sunlight brushes a bit of purple onto the clouds, and a few stars pinprick the sky.

"You and I know now," Finn continues, "that lightning is attracted to high places. Church steeples were just primitive lightning rods, before anyone knew what a lightning rod was. If God really cared, he might have pushed a few surging strokes of electrical energy a couple of metres in the other direction."

88

"So you just have terrible luck, is that it?" asks Willem.

"I wouldn't say that ancient peoples were simply experiencing bad luck when their churches got hit by lightning. After all, they did erect the steeples. The lightning didn't hit them by chance; lightning likes high places. But no one meant for it to happen, either. Neither design nor chance got those people fried."

Willem admits to himself that Heller has some compelling points of view. But he's still an asshole, and an ungrateful one. Then he remembers something. "Hey, Heller. You remember Mr. Baricco, your high school social studies teacher?"

"Yeah, sure. What about him?"

"Why'd you tell him his wife was sleeping around on him?"

"She was."

"Yeah, but how'd you know? I thought you could only see the future."

"Because I slept with her."

Willem laughs from the depths of his massive chest. "Hot damn, I knew it! What were you? Seventeen?"

"Sixteen."

"Sixteen! You must have been a god."

"You two are the only ones who know about that. I never told anyone."

"Why did you do that?" Mason asks.

"She was a very attractive woman."

Willem's laughter subsides to a low chuckle. "Heller? You're alright."

"Thanks, big man."

Often, paranoids don't sleep too well in their own beds, or beds in general. The sleeper is always vulnerable to attack. Therefore, some paranoids make a "head fake"—pillows and sheets stuffed under the blankets, to create the illusion of someone sleeping in the bed, while the paranoid finds somewhere else to sleep. Whenever Finnigan stays in a hotel room, he sleeps in the closet if it's big enough, and on the floor of the bathroom if it isn't.

The closet in Finnigan's room in the Invermere Hotel is a walk-in, and has plenty of room for him to settle down and even close the door behind him. He is about to fall asleep when someone knocks on the door.

"Yeah, just a minute," he hollers.

On the other side of the door is Penelope Mason with a paper bag in her hand. "Hey, Finn. You sleeping?"

"I guess not. What's in the bag?"

"Uh, bourbon. I got it in town yesterday. I can't sleep."

"Right, sure. Come in."

Mason enters the room and sees the bed. "Oh, I'm sorry. I didn't realize…"

"What? Oh. No, no." Finnigan pulls back the covers to reveal the body-shaped lump of pillows and sheets.

"Why did you do that?"

"It's a head fake."

"A what?"

"A head fake. Never mind. What's up?"

"You want a drink?"

"Sure."

Mason grabs two glasses from a brass tray beside the television. She pours two drinks and hands one to Finn, who sits in the only chair by the desk. "You know what?" she says, perching on the edge of the bed. He takes a sip of bourbon. "I was watching the weather channel when we were first trying to track you down. Sounds kind of stupid now, doesn't it?"

Finn smirks and tilts his head back, draining the glass. "Not really. It's a start, I guess." He holds his glass out for more bourbon, and she pours it for him while she finishes her own.

"Were you really born in a parking lot?"

"Yeah. Well, I guess they managed to get my mom into the backseat of a car. It was freezing outside."

"You really sleep with your teacher's wife?"

"I did."

"Why did you do that? I mean, really."

Finnigan swirls the bourbon around, watching the surface of the liquid form an ellipse, tracing a slight line around the inside of the glass. Some consideration follows; he shrugs and downs the drink, again holding the glass out for more. Mason fills it again.

"I had been struck the night before, I don't remember for which time. Eighth, maybe. Anyway, I looked at Baricco, the fucking prick, and I just knew he was going to go home that night and fight with his wife. Then I knew he would go home the next night, expecting to fight with her some more, only this time she'd be lying in bed, naked and dead. I didn't have any visions or anything; I couldn't have told you what the woman looked like, I just knew.

"I followed him home. He walked right in the front door and started screaming at her. No hello, no 'Hi honey, I'm home.' None of that, just right into the yelling. I didn't really hear too much, but he was on to her sleeping around on him. Then I saw her, and I knew that the next day she would go out and come home with a complete stranger. She'd pass out, and while she slept, the guy would go through the cupboards and her jewellry box and all of that, ripping her off. Only problem is, she wakes up before he's done. He panics, she makes for the phone to call the cops. He kills her.

"So, I skip school the next day, and I follow Mrs. Baricco out. Now this woman's in rough shape, I mean serious emotional problems. She doesn't even bother with singles bars or dance clubs, or any of the regular shit. She goes to the fucking supermarket in the middle of the day to find someone to screw while she buys her milk. She's not picky; she'll take just about anyone. The whole time I'm watching her I know that she's good as dead as soon as she walks down the frozen foods aisle. Then I notice she's a *babe*. I'm sixteen, and lightning or no lightning, I have hormones and they're all telling me to move in on her. Then, it's gone. She isn't dead any-more. The instant I decide to intersect her life, her future is uncertain. Instead of taking home a total psy-cho, she takes me. And lives."

"You saved her life."

"Sure, yeah."

"Do you usually help people like that?"

"By sleeping with them? Depends what they look like."

"You know what I mean."

"Sometimes, sure. Doesn't take much, usually. Most of the time, a suggestion will do it. It's hard not to."

"So, why did you insult your teacher in the middle of class?"

"Well, he was a prick and he was getting on my nerves."

Mason smiles at Finn. "You're not what I expected, that's for sure."

"That's what Willem said, too. You'll have to thank him for me."

"Why?"

"I suspect that if it wasn't for him, that other guy would have found me first. Willem sure beat the hell out of him, didn't he?"

"Yeah. You should have seen the look on his face when we made it out of the hotel. He would have killed Willem if he could have. I wonder who he is."

"Someone like you. Obsessed with me for some reason."

Mason gets up and turns out the light. She pours another drink and looks out the window. Invermere enjoys very little light pollution, and a great star field shimmers across the sky. "I'm not obsessed with you."

"Yes, you are. There is nothing you can learn from me, and you know it. Analyzing weather patterns and the whole bit might convince you, but it doesn't convince me. I'd be flattered if I wasn't so annoyed."

"You are a unique individual."

"No, Willem is a unique individual. I'm just a guy with bad luck."

"I thought you didn't believe in luck."

"Well I didn't, but the two of you might change my mind on it. You know, I've never been hit this many times in such a short time span. I think it's your fault. Day after tomorrow will be, what? Three times in two weeks?"

Mason finds that Finn is standing right next to her, almost touching her. "Sorry about that." She sets her glass down and puts her hands on his shoulders. She didn't come to this room with a bottle of bourbon for no reason.

Finn slips his left hand around her waist, and traces the bridge of her nose with his right index finger. "Have I told you that you have a pretty nose?"

"Yes. When we first met."

"Oh, right."

"Finn? Where's Ulysses?"

"He was getting bored, so I let him out for the night. He's going to find some juicy scraps behind the seafood restaurant. He'll have to beat up some neighborhood cats for it, and he'll get a couple of light scratches, but that's okay. He likes to mix it up. And he loves seafood."

"Oh."

"He'll be back around four-thirty or so. Remind me to open the window."

"Okay."

Martha Heller is seven months pregnant and unmarried. It is December 14, 1975. She is twenty-eight years old. The father of her child is long gone, and she's glad. He was a mistake she made in a nightclub, and now she's paying for that mistake.

She's passing through town on her way out to Calgary to stay with friends. Tonight, she is staying with some old friends of her parents whom she hasn't seen since her folks died.

A half-hour ago, she was wading in the pool, alone, because her friends said it was too cold to go swimming. Fairmont is safe enough for a pregnant woman to be walking through a parking lot by herself at night.

This particular winter has been mild so far, and not very much snow, which is odd in the middle of a mountain range. Martha hears a few women talking over by their car, something about the physique of some man they saw in the pool earlier.

Usually, Martha likes to look at the mountains after a swim, but tonight, a layer of dark clouds obscures them from view, and she thinks it is finally going to snow.

If she hadn't stopped to pick up the two-dollar bill in a puddle, dropped hours earlier by a seven-year-old girl who was having trouble holding her ice cream cone with one hand, Martha would have made it to her car and lived.

She feels a tingling at the base of her spine. This tingling spreads in three directions: up her spine to her neck, and through her hips and down each leg. Once the tingling reaches her neck, it splits again: one way for each arm, one way for her head. This tingling lasts for less than a second before a lightning bolt arcs through the sky and strikes her.

She is burned very badly, and her nervous system fries. The women talking by their car find her barely alive. The added trauma of premature labour is enough to kill her while giving birth to her son.

"Do you know where the safest place to be in a thunderstorm is?" asks Finn.

"No, where?"

"Your car."

"Really?"

"Yeah. Metal frame and rubber tires. Dissipates the charge perfectly."

"Finn?"

"Yeah?"

"It's almost four-thirty. You have to let Ulysses in."

In London, England, seven school children are on a field trip to the library with their young teacher. The grand old library is only across the park from their school. The children are only eight years old, so most of them do not appreciate the floor-to-ceiling shelves filled with thousands of huge volumes.

A good-sized storm is brewing, and the wind blows hard, pelting the children with freezing rain. Miss Larter has the children hold hands so no one gets lost in the storm.

They form a chain, the seven children, trailing behind their teacher who glances back every few seconds while leading them across the grassy field that separates the library from the school. The children trust her, despite her bad judgment, because she's very sweet to all of them.

Miss Larter is thinking that this is very strange weather for this time of year; it's raining when, really, it should be snowing, and a bolt of lightning hits eight-year-old Eric Able at the back of the chain. Electricity loves chains, and all seven children and poor Miss Larter are instantly at the mercy of physics. The chain of children is blown apart in a flash of blue and white light. Eric Able is the only one to survive. It is December 15, 1975.

Eric Able doesn't have to wait for long before he finds Heller and his friends. They're eating dinner together on the patio of a restaurant on a street designed to make people who have never been to Europe think of Europe. This street is part of Canadian pseudo-culture: bits and pieces of culture stolen from other parts of the world, distilled, painted over, and mashed together to create something these people call "Canadian." He can't wait to leave this country.

All the way back to their hotel, they laugh and joke with each other. This has turned into a vacation for them, and they are complacent. When Finnigan Heller is struck by lightning again, they will not be with him. This time, Eric Able will be there.

This morning, Eric Able's nose opened up enough to let in the air, and the wonderful smells of the world returned to him.

Their three separate rooms are right next to each other, and Finnigan retreats into his room first with some food for his cat. Leaving only Penelope Mason and Clyde Willem. Perfect.

Eric Able brought the lead bar to defend himself against Willem, but it will do just fine on the woman as well. Quicker than choking. He stands behind her and raises the bar above her head, readying for a blow. The hollow bar makes a dull metallic thump, but not against Mason's head. Willem, the fool, puts all his weight against her, throwing her into Able's chest and out of the way of the strike. The bar crashes down on Willem's head, cracking his skull and spattering blood across the floor.

Mason pushes against Able's chest, putting his back against the wall. "Finn!" she yells, before Able whips the bar across her face. She falls to her knees, no real damage done to her head. She's still conscious, and he swings the bar up again.

Finnigan opens his door at the sound of Mason shouting his name, and shoots his hands out to catch Eric Able's wrist. As Heller pushes him to the wall, he recognizes the man he saw bleeding at Nose Hill Park a week earlier.

Able bares his teeth and prepares to club his assailant when he realizes who it is that has him pinned against the wall.

"Finnigan Heller," Eric Able breathes.

"Who are you?"

"Eric Able. I've been searching for you."

Each man sees a connection in the other's eyes. Neither man knows what it means, but Finnigan knows that Eric Able has been struck by lightning.

"Tell me quickly what you want. They need to get to the hospital."

"Where and when?"

"Tomorrow night. Eight thirty-seven. The bridge over the creek...just off the main road."

"He has a fractured skull. Lost a lot of blood. The doctors say he's fifty/fifty." Finnigan sits beside Mason's hospital bed. She has a broken nose and a fractured cheekbone.

"Do you think he'll be okay?" Mason's voice is muffled under her bandages.

"He's going to wake up tomorrow night. He'll be very hungry and won't remember much about what happened."

"Do you...know?"

"Yes."

"Does that mean his future is beyond your influence? Because you know what's going to happen?"

"For the time being anyway."

"And me?"

"Sorry. Looks like you still have to deal with me. At least for a couple of days."

"As long as Willem is alright. I guess that's twice he saved me."

"He is the knight in shining armour type, isn't he?"

"Finn. He's not even here to defend himself."

"Sorry. Uh, I'd better get going, Mason. I have to feed Ulysses before I go up to Fairmont."

"Hey, Finn?"

"Yeah?"

Mason fiddles with her fingers. "Uh...ah forget it. It's not my style."

Finnigan sits silently at the side of her bed, looking at her bandages. Her right eye is black and swollen shut, and her other eye is darting back and forth, unable to make contact with Finn's eyes.

"Your nose will never be the same."

"What?"

"Never mind. I have to go."

"What happens if you don't go?"

"You can't separate one side of a coin from the other."

Mason nods. Finn pats her hand gently and leaves.

A short wooden bridge crosses a creek in the woods, and at eight-thirty, Finnigan Heller walks along the path, brushing against the pine trees, until he stands to one side of the bridge. The rain falls in light drops, but the heavy wind whips them into freezing pellets, shot almost horizontal from the sky. The creek seems to rush faster than usual. Eric Able is here waiting.

"I wonder if this is what Benjamin Franklin had in mind," says Finnigan.

Able says nothing. Finnigan walks across the bridge to stand before him. The rain patters on the leaves. Finnigan smells ozone before Able does.

"I know you've come a long way, Able, or whatever your

name is. But I'll tell you what I told them. I don't have the answers you're looking for. If you want to know about lightning, buy a book, and then maybe you can tell me."

Eric Able takes two steps towards Finnigan. Here is the man he has been searching for, soaking wet in the rain, standing here as if he had come across a stranger in the woods while out for a walk. Tall and wiry, Eric Able stands taller than Heller, and he can't help but feel a little disappointed at the man who represents the answer to Eric Able's question. "Can you see the future?"

"No, I can't. For some people, I just know what's going to happen."

"What will happen to me?"

Finnigan, about to tell Eric Able that he does not know the man's future, stops himself, because he realizes that he does know. No matter what Finnigan says to this man, this man obsessed with lightning, his fate will not change. "I don't think I should tell you."

A distant lightning strike precedes a ripple of thunder, momentarily drowning out the raindrops splashing into the creek. The smell of mud and sap fills the air. Finnigan clenches his fists, numb from the cold. Eric Able looks to the sky as if he is trying to will the lightning to come down, but it does not. His eyes find Finnigan's in the growing darkness. "Why aren't you hurt?" he asks.

The rain is coming down harder now, and Finnigan has to shout. "Because you didn't hit me with that lead bar of yours, you hit my friends. I may be the lightning rod, but I think your brain is fried."

"No," says Eric Able. He lifts up his shirt to show Finnigan his scar. In the failing light, Finnigan can't see the scar very well, but he knows what the mass of twisted tissue signifies. "Why don't you burn?"

Finnigan realizes what Eric wants to know, but isn't sure how to answer him. He feels a twinge of guilt at the sight of his scar. Finnigan has never had to ask himself why he was never injured, never scarred, at the searing blade of a lightning bolt. "I don't know. Look, I'm sorry if you were hurt, but I can't answer that question for you. Maybe there is such a thing as luck."

"You know that isn't true," Able says, the desperation apparent in his strained voice. He lets his shirt, wet with rain, fall back into place. He pleads, "Luck didn't bring me here. Luck doesn't bring you the lightning."

"You're right." Sheet lightning blasts right overhead, illuminating the woods with electric light. Eric Able flinches; just as the light fades, Finnigan catches the slight movement of his shoulders hunching, of his eyes squinting, and in that instant Finnigan sees that for all of Eric's desire, for all of his need, he is afraid.

One more step forward and Eric Able now stands nose-to-nose with Finnigan Heller. It is now eight thirty-five. "Tell me how. How do you get the lightning to follow you? How do you know where it will be? I have to know."

"Uncertainty."

"I don't understand."

"No one knows when or where lightning will strike, it's completely unpredictable. A billion unknown factors have to converge for lightning to hit one specific spot. You don't know what decisions you're going to make tomorrow, and that means you can't change your decisions. Your uncertainty is my inevitability."

Eric Able holds out his hands as if waiting for Finnigan to give him something. "There has to be more. I need more."

"How many times have you been struck?"

"Once. Twenty-eight years ago. It won't come back to me. I can see it, like you can, but it's always on the horizon. It runs from me."

Finnigan knows that Eric Able should be dead. Twenty-eight years ago, Eric Able was supposed to die. Just like Finnigan Heller. "An electron in the sky doesn't know where the lightning will be, it's just drawn to the place it's supposed to go to."

"Damn you, Heller. I need to know!"

And now, Finnigan Heller knows something else. "I'm sorry," Finn says, "but it's your nature. You just don't understand lightning."

An electron does not travel through space in a conventional manner. Normal particles travel from point A to point B and occupy every point in between on the journey. An electron exists at point A, and then instantaneously exists at point B, without having to travel between the two points. No one can ever calculate exactly where an electron will be, one can only define a space within which an electron is likely to appear. All of these uncertainties reduce to a single, instantaneous event; a collection of static charge which erupts at eight thirty-seven to strike Finnigan Heller for the eighteenth time. Eric Able is standing close enough that he gets struck too, and the two men fly apart; Finnigan lands on his back in the shallow creek, and Eric is thrown against the trunk of a Douglas fir.

Finnigan Heller pulls himself out of the creek, his senses heightened, his eyes aware of every single raindrop that falls before him. Seven metres away, Eric Able's inert body is twisted at the base of a tree. Finnigan rushes over to him, slipping in the thick mud, and catches a new scent with his augmented sense of smell; that of smoldering flesh.

Finnigan gently pulls Able out from underneath the tree. Every last bit of hair on his head is gone, even his eyebrows and eyelashes. Finnigan reaches down to Eric's wrist to check his pulse, and burns his finger on the metal watchstrap, which is now fused to his wrist. The raindrops landing on Able's head collect in the blackened cracks on his burned face. His nervous system, snarled and overloaded from the lightning, shuts down, but for a few seconds he focusses on an invisible object behind Finnigan's head. Finnigan thinks that Eric's eyes are blind, that they cannot see, but then he notices that they are looking at something farther off, not in space, but in time. A sparse breath passes between Eric Able's charred and blackened lips, carrying the words, "You will…" but he dies before he can finish the sentence.

Finnigan Heller knows the future. As the seconds tick away following the latest lightning bolt, he sees an infinite divergence of possibilities, even about his own future, because he does not yet know what he will decide to do. The rain wraps around his bowed head and pours to the mud at his feet, flowing in rivulets downhill to the edge of the creek, coaxed by gravity into the path of least resistance.

The possibilities fade however, and as Finnigan tries to grasp on to just one, he finds them slipping away even faster. He runs his shaking fingers through his soaked hair. Another lightning bolt flashes far off to the north, and the brisk wall of a thunderclap slams around Finnigan, waking him to where he is. Eric Able's body lies in the mud, exactly where it will be found early tomorrow morning by an elderly man out for a walk, who will come across the body as he stumbles in the thick, wet earth. The man will not be troubled by the discovery, but will walk across the bridge over the creek, along the path through the woods, and down the road to the first house he sees. Once there, he will call an ambulance, and then leave.

"It's a real shame," says Finnigan in Mason's hospital room. She looks around the room, looking for anything she might have forgotten. In the bed on the other side of the room lies a young man, injured when his boat capsized on the lake. His girlfriend sits beside him and reads a magazine. In the oval mirror on the wall, Mason examines the bandage over her nose. Finnigan looks into the mirror from over her shoulder, peering at the bandage as if he can see through it.

"What do you mean? It's fine now."

"It's going to be crooked."

"Are you reading my nose's future?" Mason turns around and glares at Finn, who reaches out to touch the bandage.

"No, I can tell through the bandage. It's crooked." Ulysses creeps out from under Finn's long coat and meows. "Ulysses agrees."

"I'll get over it."

"Oh, I brought you something. You can add it to your little file you have on me." Finn hands Ulysses to Mason and reaches into the inside pocket of his coat. "Here," he says, handing her a newspaper clipping. Mason takes it and, after setting Ulysses down on the bed, reads the headline, Man Killed in Lightning Strike.

Mason sits on the bed and scans the article. "I wonder," she says, "am I going to have to close that file?" Finn looks through the mirror at the woman reading the magazine on the other side of the room. In three hours, her boyfriend will wake up from his nap, and they will argue about the accident.

Finn says, "That wasn't the last lightning bolt, if that's

what you mean. Not for me." He turns around and walks over to the woman reading the magazine. A thin strand of light brown hair falls from her ponytail and brushes the page she turns. Her face looks relaxed and calm, but her fingertips tremble, and her eyes, Finn notices, don't follow the words on the page. "Don't worry," he says. The young woman looks up at him, angry that her privacy has been disturbed. She grabs the strand of hair that has fallen in her face and jams it behind her ear. Before she can reply, Finn says, "He'll wake up soon."

As they leave the hospital, Mason asks, "What was he looking for?"

A wisp of white cloud, all that is left from the heavy sky the night before, passes across the sun, and then breaks away. Finn takes his sunglasses out from his breast pocket and slips them over his eyes. Ulysses purrs from his place in the crook of Finn's elbow. "He wanted what I have."

"A gift for attracting a zillion volts of electricity? Yeah, I sure envy you."

"You were following me too."

"Yeah, but I wasn't looking to get zapped by lightning."

Finn shakes his head. "No, it was something different. He wanted to know it was coming, like I do. And I think, before he died, he did know."

"How so? Did he tell you your future?"

"I think he was trying to." Finn falls silent, and scratches

Ulysses' belly with his free hand. Mason walks beside him, also silent, occasionally looking over at him, studying his face in profile; the hard line of his jaw with a day of stubble, the curve of his nose under his wraparound sunglasses. She can't see his eyes underneath the tinted glass, but to her he appears to be scanning all of the people around him: a mother quickly pushing a stroller across the street, two children playing with plastic trucks in a sandbox in a park, an elderly couple holding hands ahead of them on the sidewalk. Mason imagines the possibilities that must be unfolding for Finn now, all formulating in his head just as easily as she can picture an apple or a cup of coffee.

On a hill overlooking the lake, Finn sits on a wooden bench facing the water. Ulysses leaps to the grass and prowls around a nearby garbage can.

"If I know your future," says Finn, "I can change it. But if he knew my future, did he change it? Did he change it just by telling me he knew?" Finn holds his hands out, as if he's not only speaking to Mason, but to the surroundings. Ulysses takes his gesture as a sign to jump into Finn's lap. Mason scratches behind the cat's half-ear.

"Maybe he was trying to help you. That's what you do, isn't it?"

"I thought I was just the asshole drifter."

"That's what Willem thinks. I think you were starting to grow on him though, until he got bashed in the head with a pipe. We should go check on him, I think."

Ulysses meows. Finn rustles the cat's whiskers, and

Ulysses bites and claws playfully at Finn's finger. "Right, that sounds like fun." He waves a hand in the air. "You go ahead, I think I'll start walking to the coast."

"Do you have a lightning strike planned?"

"No, I just think I'd like to see the ocean. How about a ride to the bus station?"

Mason turns on the bench to face him. She reaches to remove his sunglasses, but decides not to, and instead straightens the collar of his jacket. "Want to come back east with us? I could put you in the lab, run some tests, hook you up to my car in the winter?"

Finn stands up, lifting Ulysses with him. "That's alright, I'm happy enough that no one's following me anymore. But read the newspaper in seven months and three days. I might be in the neighbourhood." Finn walks down the hill, towards the lake. Mason smirks and shakes her head. The smile makes her broken nose ache, and her eyes water. "Oh, and," says Finn, turning around, "tell Willem not to use the bourbon trick again when you're back in Calgary. He really won't do well with another concussion."

Mason stands up and smiles wider, sending sharp needles of pain into her nose. Her eyes water, and tears wet her cheeks. She's sure Finn sees them before they're soaked up by her bandage, but she only smiles harder. "See you around, Heller," she calls after him.

He waves and turns back towards the lake. "You just might."

Geoffrey Bromhead was born in Calgary, Alberta in 1979. He currently studies English literature and creative writing at the University of Calgary. *Struck* is his first published novel.